Sherlock Holmes

Urban Fantasy Mysteries 4

John Pirillo

Lovecraft

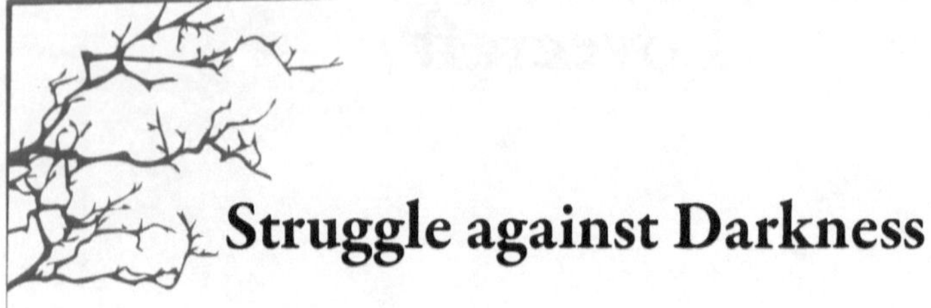

Struggle against Darkness

"No!" Harry cried out as he thrust at the darkness threatening to engulf him.

It was not palpable in the sense of being a substantial life form, like a human being or even some magical creature. No, it was thick and void, like those mysterious parts of the galaxy that scientists like Nikola Tesla and Thomas Edison were guessing exhibited strange behavior, like garbage cans in space, sucking in all matter.

He had asked Merlin once about such things and Merlin would say nothing any more definite than that one-day Harry would divine their purpose. Whether for good or for evil.

The Ritual of Horror

H.P. Lovecraft listened to his wife and child play in the common room and smiled. He would have loved to join them. Usually, he did. But this afternoon he had a deadline to meet.

The London Literary Journal was publishing his latest story: "A Meeting of Man with the Elder Gods." It was his latest attempt at describing the outer dimensions he had learned of during his visit to ancient India, where tribesmen spoke of monsters and demons...Rakshasas, who terrorized the countryside and summoned by certain spells and books.

He had spent two years studying the myths and legends of that area of the world and eventually branched out to other countries nearby. But the length and the breadth of his studies assured him of one thing and one thing only...that man's ability to imagine anything from the uttermost sublime to the horrifying depths of terror was the same everywhere.

When he returned home from his travels he returned to his home with Evelyn, a lovely woman of determined spirit, whom he wished to be the mother of his children, as well as the pride of his life. Books were well and good, but a warm hand at night to hold and an arm body to cozy with on a long walk in the mornings was worth more than any fortune in the world.

Still, he had to pay the bills.

So, there he was conjuring up another spell to add to his latest story. This was one that he remembered from his travels. To this point in time, he had refused to put such on paper, let alone speak it aloud. But this was no time to be squeamish or condescending about what he had heard.

He needed it. So, he began reciting the ritual aloud as he wrote it down, changing certain words to make it more terrifying as he did so.

He was desperate to put something unusual on paper to hold his readers attention. He knew this would be it. In fact, he could feel it in his bones and every cell of his body.

As he began writing his thoughts down and the ritual for summoning the Elder Gods, he felt a tension building about him.

At first, he thought an approaching storm was electrifying the atmosphere. He could still hear his wife and child playing together. So, he went to the study windows and flung them open.

The outside was calm and peaceful as it usually was

this time of day. Not a cloud in sight.

But the tension and dryness of the air seemed growing. He turned about and found his paperwork giving off an odd mirage like shivering of the air, as if he were traveling the Great Deserts and not standing amid a London home.

The shivering increased and then a foul odor began to build. He coughed from the stink and foulness of its scent, plucked his handkerchief out to cover his nose.

The shivering continued and began to expand. The papers fluttered to the floor, but in a certain pattern.

He froze the moment he saw it: the pattern of the Elder Gods! Two triangles opposing each other. Rising as if on the forehead of some invisible creature.

Then before he could flee the room, the windows slammed shut with a loud bang.

The sound of his wife and child were lost as something straight from the tales of horror he had heard in India began to step forth from the shivering air above his paperwork.

But it did not stop entering. It just kept growing and growing and...

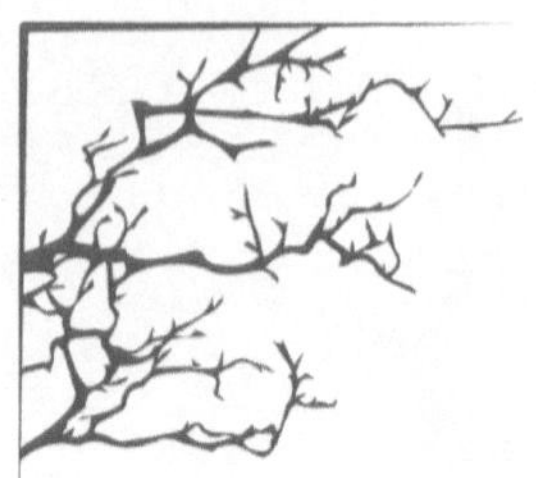

Evil Strikes

She walked quickly along Henley Street, the dimming light of the setting sun casting golden rods of light upon her heavy coat. She shivered a moment, and then pulled her wrap tighter about her throat. The scarf was handmade from wool and cotton she had sewn together by hand in her spare time. Of which she seemed to have less and less to spare these days.

She sighed.

Soon she would be home to her family.

Her husband.

She frowned when that word popped into her mind.

He really was not the sort she wanted to come home to.

Not anymore. Something about him had changed. It was as if he were another man altogether. Something emerged from him that frightened her. This kept her spending more time at social functions so she would not have to be alone with him any longer than she had to.

When he touched her now, she felt violated, as if his fingers were not of human flesh, but something disgusting and unclean. She always had to take a bath or scrub where he had touched her soon afterwards or she would feel unclean for the rest of the day or night.

It was starting to wear her down; but she did not know what to do about it. A woman's place was with her family, with her man. But...then all that had changed. All that had changed drastically.

SHE HAD FOUND HIM GROPING the maid the other day behind the dressing curtains, when he thought she was out of the house. And she would still have missed it if her daughter, Kathryn, had not come running to her where she was in the garden and giggled, "Daddy's playing with Gertrude's bottom again."

She gave Kathryn a shocked look, and then rushed inside, up the two flights of stairs and into their oversized bedroom.

And sure enough, the scoundrel not only had his hands in her pants, but something else that he had used to bring Kathryn into this world.

He was moaning with pleasure when he heard the door slam shut behind her.

"Gertrude!"

The maid lay on her bed, still moaning with pleasure, not with it for some reason. As if she weren't quite in her body somehow. Her eyes were spools of pure white, the color completely gone from them, and her flesh appeared clammy and wet, as if she had taken a bath in scum.

She had given her husband a long look. "When I return from the society meeting, Gertrude will no longer be in our house!"

He had said nothing. Just stood there with his pants hanging about his ankles, as if it were something he did all the time. And something else was hanging down between his legs, but it should not have been there. Not on him, not on any man that lived in her world. But he was her first man, so what did she know, except by what the other ladies discussed quite discreetly in the meetings she attended.

She was shaken at the time. Gave it no further thought, but instead, wanting to scream at the top of her lungs in anger and frustration, she fled the bedroom for the sanctity of the lower part of her house.

There she found Kathryn reaching the stairs, giggling. "Did you see, Mommy, did you see?"

She shook her head, rushed downstairs and caught Kathryn up in her arms. "You're staying with Grandma!"

"But Mommy, Daddy is so funny! Want to watch some more, I..."

Evelyn clamped a hand over her daughter's mouth. "Do not ever, ever mention this again to anyone. Not me. Not your grandmother, not anyone, do you understand?"

The little girl nodded, as tears pooled in the corners of her eyes, then she burst into real tears and began sobbing.

Evelyn felt her heart break. Her daughter should not have had to endure what she had just thrust upon her. Now she felt not only angry at him and Gertrude, but at herself. As well as scared and horrified. She was also beginning to wish she had never been born. And she was not the kind of person who ever thought negatively like that.

AND THAT WAS ONLY THE beginning of her dreadful day.

"I'M AFRAID, MADAME Barry, that your services as our society's treasurer are no longer needed."

Evelyn Barry, already distraught from the morning's revelations, felt as if her heart was ripped from her chest. "Wha...what?"

The President of the Society Madams of London
gave her a stern look. "It has come to our attention that funds have been missing from the account."

She gave Evelyn a pointed look. "Funds which you were to have deposited."

"But I did..." She started to say, then froze. "Which day?"

The President gave her a surprised look. "Which day? What does it matter which day, missing funds are quite inappropriate no matter which day," she scolded Evelyn.

Evelyn shoved her face into that of the older woman's. "Which day, drat it all?"

IT WAS HER HUSBAND. He had reported the missing funds found in their account. How could he do such a thing? Why? What could he have to gain from such a cowardly and treacherous thing? She could still end up behind bars as if the Society voted to do so. She shivered at the prospect of spending the rest of her days behind bars in a dank, dark prison cell. The Queen was quite harsh on those who robbed from the poor. And she was accused of doing just such a thing.

She looked up from the sidewalk where shadows were covering the pimples and pocks of way too many heavy carts drawn along them. The local merchants used the sidewalks like roads to cart their merchandise from the warehouse four blocks down. This is how Evelyn had been able to buy the nice house they now had at a steep discount. No one wanted to live in such an uncouth environment.

She did not care. She loved the common person, finding them uncommonly interesting. And now today, even more so, since her husband, who was the head of a local bank, should have been much less common, and had turned out to be quite common indeed! No, not common at all, but less than the vermin that swarmed in the sewers of London.

Were she not a lady, then at that thought, she would have spat to rid the sour taste the vision of him brought forth into her consciousness.

She frowned as her home came into view.

What home?

She had deliberately avoided seeing her mother right after she lost her job. She had enough to explain that her husband was an adulterer; but now that he was also a thief! She shuddered at the horror of it all.

But as she neared the home, she had forgotten to check the alleyway that cut between the two blocks of her path. She usually stepped out into the street some to keep further from them, knowing that the cheap crooks, thieves, and muggers found them to be their best hiding places for mischief.

And this day she wanted no further mischief.

But she had not looked.

Something grabbed her by the throat.

Before she could scream, she was grabbed to safety, yanked from the street into the alleyway and slammed against its wall.

She looked on in horror at something out of her worst nightmare.

Her husband!

But not as he should have looked at all.

As he opened his mouth in a grin that caused every single part of her body to scream in terror, she had only one thought. "Poor Kathryn!"

Her husband smiled, and her terror increased as he said, "I have something to show you. Something incredibly special!"

Then he showed her.

Her scream woke up every animal for blocks, started cats howling and dogs barking.

Neighbors shuttered their windows with slams.

Pedestrians out late scurried for the safety of the nearest door.

Then one more scream broke the night. And this one seemed to go on forever.

Then abruptly stopped!

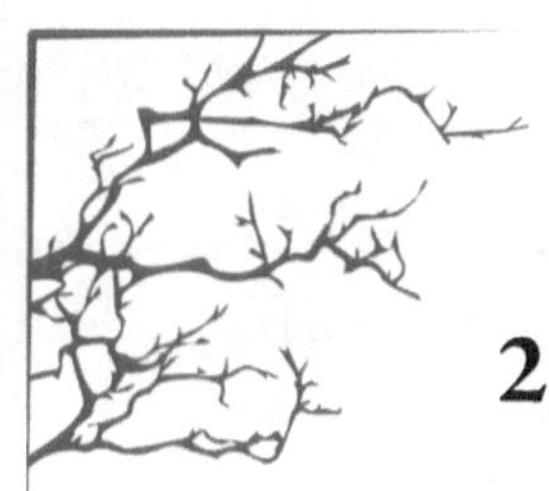

221 B Baker Street

"Really, Harry, is that the best you can do?" Watson demanded as he completed the taking of Harry's Bishop with his Queen.

"Checkmate!" Watson declared next.

Harry sighed and pushed the board away from them.

"I'm sorry, Watson, I'm a bit distracted today."

"No wonder," Watson remarked, a twinkle in his eyes. "Your stomach is still fluttering over that incident. Mine would."

Holmes looked up from Conan's latest book, "The Adventures of Steampunk Holmes," an amused look curling his lips.

"A new transformation in the mix, hey Harry?"

Harry got up and went to the doorway to the sitting room and sighed. "Would hardly call getting beat by Watson a new transformation, Holmes."

Holmes laughed. "I'm sure Watson would."

Harry turned to favor his friend with a smile. "I'm sure he would."

Watson grinned back at him, but Harry had already turned his back from his friends again. Things were bothering him. He had not the heart to tell Watson he had let him win so he could have a bit more time to ponder what was bothering him.

"Then again, Harry," Holmes went on. "Perhaps a new game's afoot that is not necessarily criminal."

Harry, still paused in the doorway, pondered the question, as it had at least two other levels to it. He was one of the few men, not knowing Holmes well yet, who could fathom his oftentimes layered remarks.

Harry sat down at the table with Watson, who at once scooted over a plate of scones towards him, then a pot of tea.

"Bit cool now, but rather good despite it," Watson said in an endearing voice.

Harry absent-mindedly scooped a scone onto a small China saucer, then took the pot and poured a tiny bit of tea into a matching cup, added honey from a pot in the center of the table, then took a spoon from the napkin that Watson hurriedly slid to him and stirred it.

"Thanks Watson."

Watson nodded and gave Harry a questioning look.

Harry finally answered Holmes's question. The tea did work anyway, even if to cool, to settle his nerves.

"I'm sure you haven't heard all the details yet of the

new case that Challenger, Conan and I are working on." Harry commented, knowing that would tweak Holmes's curiosity if he did not.

Holmes obligingly laid his book open face down on his lap and curled his hands over it to listen.

"So, you have actually begun your detective work as a team then?"

Harry smiled momentarily as he saw the name in his mind. "Got it from you, Holmes. So, I suppose I, we owe you for that."

"What is it?"

"The Crystal Deduction."

Watson clapped his hands. "Bravo, Harry. It is as exciting as the magical performances you regularly give at the Globe."

Harry shook his head. "But much more dangerous. We have already been chased by werewolves, distraught vampire wives and a leprechaun that hid pots of gold in the bathrooms of rich people and then ate them."

"The gold, Harry?" Watson asked.

"That too," Harry replied.

"Oh dear," Watson said, not liking the image that brought forth into his mind.

"Holmes," Harry asked.

"Yes?"

"There are rumors of some kind of beast roaming the streets of London," Harry announced.

"What does that have to do with a transformation?"

Harry considered that a moment, then replied, "Every major change my powers have gone through have always been preceded by some kind of event that forces me to draw on powers I didn't know I had yet."

"See, and then you feel this...uh...beast...could be the provider of more power to you?"

Harry, exasperated with the questioning, spoke up, "Holmes, I am merely recounting the facts, not conjecturing or conjuring the future."

Holmes nodded. "Apologize, Harry. Merely trying to point out that perhaps you drive yourself too hard for perfection, when it's really a quality that comes with time and patience."

"I've never been known to be a patient man, Holmes," Harry replied.

Holmes smiled lightly. "Perhaps, but you're still alive, are you not?"

Watson caught on at once when Harry's face went blank for a moment. "For heaven's sake, Harry, your magical acts are hellishly more dangerous than most monsters we hunt; and you somehow manage to escape them quite readily. Your magical plights, I mean."

"That's because I prepare for them over and over and..."

Harry stopped himself. He got it finally. "See what you're getting at. Magic is no different."

Holmes saw no need to agree or disagree, he picked up his book once more to read it, "Curious villain in this version," he pointed out to nobody.

"How so, Holmes?" Watson asked out of curiosity.

Holmes put a finger on a couple of words to imprint them firmly in his memory, and then traced the words to a series of triangular symbols on the page.

He had a perfect memory, but when he did what he had just done, it made those words pop back into his mind at the proper time of reference...such as a specific moment of solving a case, or in a moment of dire need. But the image would stick in his mind without much effort. It recalled to him something he wished he could forget about from his own world. A certain person as well. One, whom he hoped, prayed was as dead as he had left him. Or thought him to be.

It was a lingering fear of Holmes that the man was

still alive and would return to haunt him once more. A fear that struck him to the very core and left him wakeful many a night, broken out into a cold sweat.

If not for his training by the Monk, the worries and fears might have permanently disabled him, or at the very least weakened the keenness of his mind.

"Lovecraft is a great author and a close friend of Conan's, is he not?"

Watson nodded. "Yes, I met him just the other day at a party thrown at Lord Graystone's. Lovely chap. Bit gray at the temples for his age and has a very peculiar lump at the back of his neck which he constantly rubs at, but otherwise normal as a pickle in a sandwich."

Watson stabbed a new scone to eat. "Asked him to see me privately so I can examine the lump more closely, but so far he has not communicated with me."

"He uses the lump for inspiration in his stories. They deal so much with the dark and diabolical."

"That wouldn't surprise me," Watson agreed. "And may be why he has not spoken to me again. But I do not find him to be that morbid, Harry. Quite the contrary, he has a sparkling sense of humor which is always refreshing to be about.

Holmes laughed. "How quaint, but this version of

Lovecraft is quite diabolical. I do believe Conan has produced a villain to rival Moriarty."

Watson felt a cold shiver run up and down his spine. He tried to shake it off as a coincidence until Holmes said, "And he mentions that the man utilizes creatures of a supernatural or extra supernatural nature to perform his murders."

Watson knew then what was bothering him. "Holmes, I think you and I need to take a trip to Scotland Yard."

Holmes arched an eyebrow as Watson stood up and went for the coat rack.

Watson started putting on his coat and hat and looked to Harry. "I think you also might find these fits into your agenda of challenges and transformations, Harry."

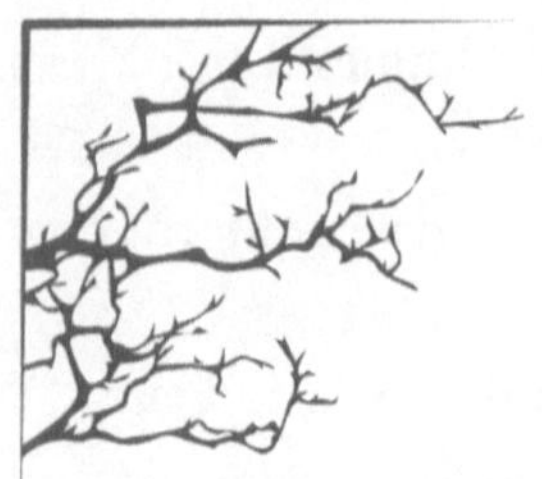

Scotland Yard

"Lady Evelyn Barry was quite eccentric, but well beloved by the members of her society," Inspector Bloodstone explained as his son pulled out the long metal drawer inside the morgue, which held her body, covered up by a sheet.

"The only odd thing about her life, or unusual, was the man to whom she was married. A writer. You know the sort, Watson, always thinking about something to cause our hearts to palpitate in fear and all."

Watson took the sheet and gently pulled it down to the crest of her breasts, but no further in respect of her femininity.

Watson ignored the dig at his own writing abilities and pointed at the woman's throat.

"See this, Holmes," Watson said, pointing to several marks upon her throat. "At first I thought, these appear to be the marks of some kind of leech, but leeches have but one mouth, not multiple mouths."

Harry dawdled to the side, reluctant to look, but knowing he must if he wished to strengthen his abilities of observation which he was learning from Holmes. He finally crept closer, reluctantly, but closer still until he was shoulder to shoulder with Watson, who pressed a gloved finger to the first of several puckered wounds upon the woman's throat.

"See here," he touched the first, "...And here," and touching two more rapidly, "...and the last."

Harry frowned deeply. It was mortifying to see such a handsome woman's face so disfigured by such a beastly mark. Her body was cold as ice now from the morgue cooler, but even in death he could tell she had flawless skin at one time and a remarkable beauty...coupled with an enthusiastic sense of humor. Her laugh lines were prominent.

"It doesn't look like a leech mark at all," Harry finally spoke out, fearful of putting to words what his emotions radiated at that moment.

Everyone turned to eye him.

Harry slipped the magic wand he always sheathed in its holster on his belt into his right hand and touched its tip to the wounds. They began to glow, at first a bright red and then the wounds began to keep puckering wider and wider.

"Yipes!" Watson cried out, backing up so quickly he slammed into Inspector Bloodstone.

Holmes and Harry were resolute as they spied the

tiny creatures begin to crawl up and out of the puckered throats of the six wounds.

"Mother Mary help us!" The Inspector said finally, crossing himself repeatedly.

"Quickly, my vials, Watson!" Holmes cried out.

Watson snapped out of his shock and hefted his black bag onto the metal drawer's flat surface, opened it and retrieved six vials.

Holmes grabbed a pair of forceps from the top of the bag, and then plucked the first tiny creature before it could crawl all the way out. It was long as a worm, but with tiny arms and legs. It had a face. Grotesque and mutilated.

He swiftly jammed its mutated body into the throat of the first vial and quickly stoppered it.

He repeated the process to the second one, but the third seemed to burst forth. It slammed into Holmes's chest, where his vest caught on fire at once as it began burning a hole in it with fluid exuded from its throat.

Harry took his magic wand to it and cried out, "Ignaceous!"

The creature burst into blue flames and fell away from Holmes to the floor.

Watson stomped on it and then stepped back.

The creature seemed to reinflate itself and move again.

Inspector Bloodstone took his nightstick to it over and over, spattering matter all over his cuffs and hands.

"That should do it!" He spoke.

Then the pieces flew back together, and the creature began darting for the doorway out.

Harry pointed his wand at it. "Ignaceous forte!" He shouted.

The creature let out a screech many times louder than it should have been capable. So loud that the men had to clap hands over their ears as the tiny thing swelled up like a balloon and then exploded into particles of glowing blue dust which evaporated into the air.

Watson eyed the stained floor, the woman's throat, the two worms in the vials that Holmes had somehow managed to hang onto and said, "I'd fancy a bit of something to eat right about now."

He took the vials, placed them into a larger bottle he always kept and then poured a preservative into it and shut it closed.

"But the sight of these doesn't bring very lovely visions of food at alright at this moment."

Holmes looked at Harry. "Well done."

Harry had no reply. He knew what they were dealing with. And from the look in Holmes eyes, he suspected he did as well.

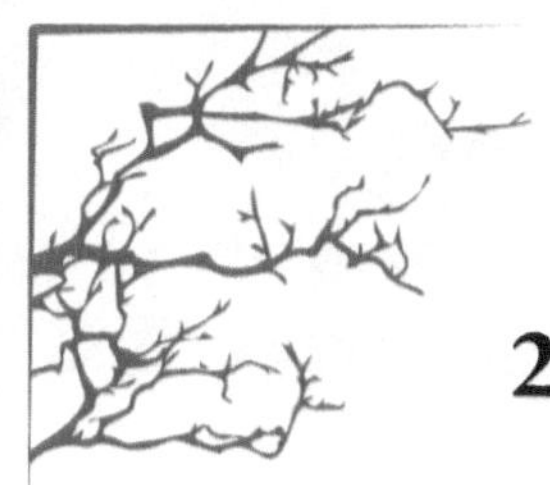

221B Baker Street

Watson and Holmes sat next to each other by the fireplace, which Watson kept stoking the fire higher and higher with more wood.

"Warm enough yet, Watson?"

"Not until I can burn the memory of that horrid thing from my mind," Watson replied.

Satisfied at last, he put his poker back against the fireplace mantle and then sighed. He turned to Holmes. "You're awfully calm about an incident that could have cost your life."

Holmes shrugged. "All in a day's work, Watson. We've both seen worse."

"Maybe. But each time seems no easier than the last, and always just as deadly."

Holmes had to agree with that, but his training told him that it did no good to dwell on the past. One had to know when to let go and move on. Such was this moment.

"I wonder how Harry is handling it."

"That worries me, Watson."

"How so?"

"Harry is younger than you and I and still untested
in many ways. His magic is strong; I will give him that, but he still lacks the maturity and patience of his mentor."

"Merlin?"

"Yes."

Watson gave Holmes a curious look. "You act as if the two of you had been consulting one another over Harry."

Holmes just smiled.

1212 Memory Lane

"Challenger, you would not believe the nature of the woman's death," Harry almost hollered from the table he and his friends were playing cards at.

Conan peeked over his hand of cards at Harry. "You sound angry, why?"

"Because a lovely woman was violated in the most disgusting of ways," Harry argued.

Challenger snorted. "As if there were a polite way of violating one."

Harry threw his cards down. "Look, we've got to get to the bottom of this before anyone else is harmed."

Conan set his cards down. He was losing badly and did not mind passing on the opportunity to show just how badly. "You have hinted at this all evening, so why not just tell us, Harry, it is obviously on your mind. A lot!"

Challenger nodded. He set his cards down. "I am tired of winning anyway. A nice story would break up the tedium of it all."

Conan glared at him.

Challenger touched his friend's arm lightly. "No harm intended, Conan, my dear friend. Love winning over you, but even a great mind like mine needs to relax once in a while."

Conan glared even harder. "Now you're starting to sound like Steampunk!"

Challenger lost his grin. "Oh. That bad, huh?"

"Worse," Harry and Conan replied at the same time.

Challenger sighed. "Stand corrected, gentlemen." He looked to Harry. "Very well, I concur with Conan, what is it that's causing you to lose your normal patience, Harry?"

Harry smiled with relief. "I believe that we are being invaded from the Dark Dimensions."

Conan sat up straight suddenly and tightened his lips together, then said, "Dark..."

"...Dimensions, that's right, you heard me correctly, Conan."

Conan frowned. "But that's just something I threw out in my last novel for the fun of it."

Harry shook his head. "You know anything's possible, Conan. Heaven knows we have been fighting with such for years now."

Conan nodded. "True enough, but never anything as frightening as the Dark Dimensions."

"That is because when we are engaged with our

enemies, we never pause to think just how horrible and disgusting those people or creatures are. We just try to win through and save those we are helping."

"And more often than not," Challenger interrupted, "Ourselves as well."

"Agreed," Harry said.

"Then you think this case might be related to the beast we've been chasing through the alleyways of London for the Inspector?"

"I do," Harry said with finality.

Challenger's eyebrows rose in thought.

Conan lifted his coffee cup and sipped some. "Cold."

Harry smiled. Slipped his magic wand from its holster on his belt and touched the cup in Conan's hands. "Warm," he said in Latin.

The cup warmed in Conan's hands and a light steam began to emit from its throat.

Conan smiled. "There are nights when I could use that warmer of yours, Harry."

Harry smiled back. "Spend ten years with me and I'll teach you how to do it yourself."

"Shah!" Conan shot back. "I'm much too old for that sort of thing."

Challenger roared with laughter.

Conan gave him a nasty look. "What's so blasted funny?"

"You finally admitting that you're an old man," Challenger hurled back at him.

Conan stood up. "Not old man. Merely an aging one."

Harry hid his smile when Conan looked to him and sat down again. "You still haven't told us what's bothering you."

None of them were that old. But after all the adventures they had been through, sometimes the weight and oppression of the violence and horrors they had to deal with weighed heavily upon their souls.

Harry tapped the lip of his coffee cup several times and it began making a ringing tone, as if someone were using it like a bell, over and over and over.

"She had three puncture marks on her throat. Equidistant and distended."

"Oh, three is nothing to worry about," Challenger pointed out smugly.

"And three more opposing those three," Harry finished.

"Oh dear," Challenger remarked, losing the grin from his face.

"How distended?" Conan asked, fascinated with the prognosis.

Harry held two fingers in a tiny circle.

Even Challenger was shook by what that made him visualize.

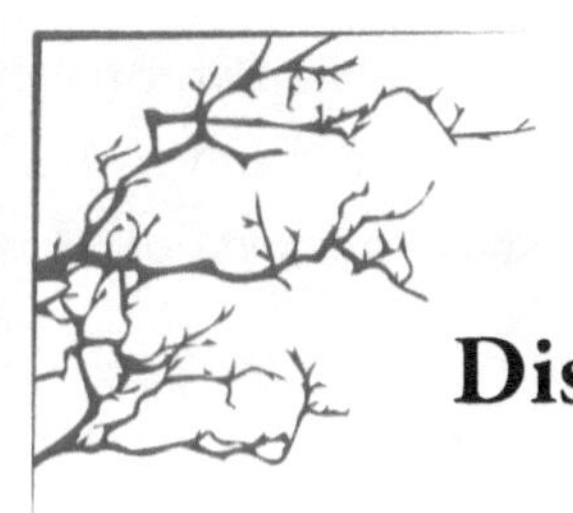

Distant Remarks and Occupations

Harry sat alongside several other young children while Merlin did parlor tricks for them. He held his cap in one hand and a stick of wood, noticeably short with a leaf at its tip in the other. The stick was his wand and, despite being severed from the tree it had been taken from, was growing longer and thicker as time went by.

"Up and out!" Merlin cried out.

A flash of smoke erupted from his cap.

Merlin made a face as the smoke went into his eyes.

The kids broke into laughter.

Merlin smiled and then reached into the cap. "Well, if you won't come out on your own, my shy little friend, then perhaps I'll give you a helping hand."

Merlin pulled out a tiny dragon. It spit at him as he gripped it behind the nape of its neck so it could not bite him.

"Whoa!" Harry cooed. "That's incredible."

The dragon suddenly scratched Merlin's thumb with its rear leg claws.

Merlin flinched enough for the dragon to break free of his hold and bite the tip of the webbing of his hand.

"Oh dear!" Merlin cried out in alarm.

He let it go and it shot off like a miniature comet into the sky, emitting a fire trail behind it.

Merlin waved at the departing dragon and shouted, "Please tell your mother I miss her."

Merlin turned to his students. "Word to the wise, when you have something that can bite you even when you have it clasped firmly by the back of the neck, then you'd best make sure you keep your eyes on the rest of the foul beast, or you'll surely regret it!"

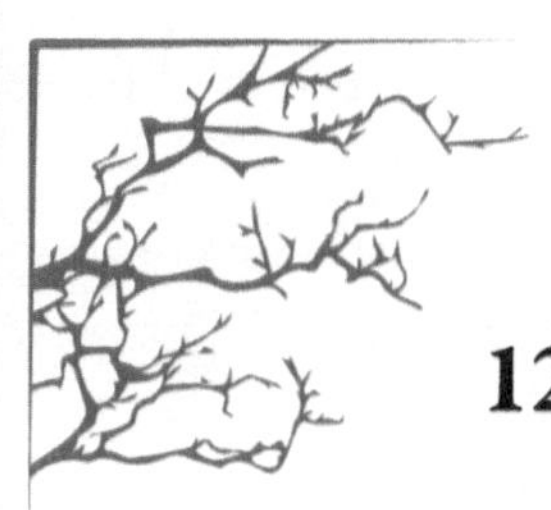

1212 Memory Lane

Harry shook his head a moment to clear the memories playing in his mind. Why that one? What wasn't he holding properly in this incident?

"And after Watson stomped on it, the Inspector smashed it to a pulp and bits, but then it came right back together again and we only stopped it when I used one of my strongest spells to dispel its magical forces," Harry told his friends.

"Well, that served the bugger right, didn't it?" Challenger acknowledged his friend's story.

"Well, actually that didn't kill it," Harry responded.

Conan looked worried. "It did not get free, did it? I really hate worms."

"Yes, I agree, Conan," Challenger added. "Especially ones from the Dark Dimension."

Harry shook his head. "We don't know that for certain yet."

"Wait," Conan stopped Harry before he could speak further. "It wasn't dead?"

Harry looked about as if someone might be over listening to them. "Don't tell Homes and Watson, and especially don't tell the Inspector, but after they left the morgue, I stayed a bit longer, pretending to attend to something I had lost there."

"Why in the world would you like that, Harry?" Challenger demanded, truly puzzled by this aspect of the story.

Harry frowned deeply in remembrance of what had happened next. "The creature reassembled itself yet again. Suspected this and a good thing I did, or else it would have gotten loose, and any amount of harm could have happened to those in the building."

"What did you do?" Conan asked, puzzled at this turn of events.

"Grabbed it by the nape of its neck, feet, and arms, and then tossed it into the crematorium, which was burning bones at that moment."

"And that destroyed it?" Challenger demanded.

"I truly hope so," Harry replied with a shred of doubt clouding his mind. "I truly do."

Challenger chewed on his lower lip for a moment in thought. "This is quite remarkable. For a creature of that size to be so hardy, then were it to fully grow up..."

"It would be absolutely deadly," Harry finished for him.

Conan spoke what was on all their minds at that

moment. "Then let us pray that the crematorium did indeed finish the job."

"Amen that!" Challenger added.

Harry, however, said another kind of prayer, a magical one, but was not sure if even that would be enough if they were all wrong.

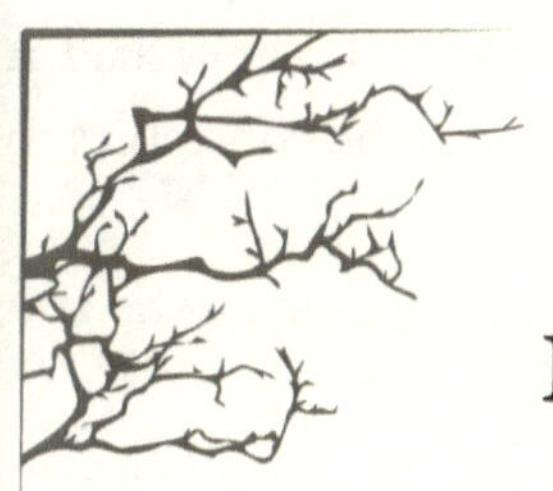

Baking Narrows

Baking Narrows is a tiny offshoot of Marley, where the business district intertwines with the distended walkways of the wharves along the Thames. It is a very well-off area, and few beggars and thieves frequent it as the better off usually have guards with them and beggars and thieves are lazy to begin with and would rather go after the easy victims than possibly lose a hand or life for their living.

"Oh, whistle my lady,
Whistle my lad,
Surely happy
Surely glad.
A good evening of luxury
In the lap of my love
Will surely bring heavenly
Sweets to my dove."

Nicholas Bayard grinned at the true meaning of his often-sung tune. He had made it up for a Midnight Angel, who lived off Baking Narrows, above the bakery two flats down near the residential area.

There she would teach him about things of warmth and pleasure, and he would share songs and advice about merchant ships and battles with sea monsters on the oceans and seas.

Naturally, she was awed by his tales, believing every one of them. Only half were true and that was enough to give his voice credibility and strength to his exaggerations when he produced them.

He looked forward to another tale or two this night and some more lessons in relaxation and pleasure by his Midnight Angel.

"Charlie," she called him.

She called everyone Charlie. She never memorized a name. Said it was too shallow. Made it too easy if she were caught by the constables to give up their names to their mistresses.

She never stayed in jail. The constables loved her as much as he and often visited her right after he left, when their shifts were over.

But tonight, she was all his. He had booked her friendship in advance and was looking forward to it. He had been wood and sea bound for nearly three months on the stretch from the Americas to London and looked forward very much to letting go of all the stress and fatigue he had built up.

He and his crew had narrowly avoided a plunge into

Davy Jones locker by a huge undersea monster that resented ships crossing its territory and only the friendly hand of Captain Nemo…who had since his long battles against the martial ships of the nations, been a changed man and a kinder and more benevolent one…had saved their ship and crew. It was one time of terror he would carry with him to his dying days. Nothing was likely to be more frightening than a hydra headed squid with the ability to turn you to stone as it sang like the beautiful mermaids that frequented that area of the world and lured them to their deaths.

"Good thing that fellow is friends with Sherlock Homes, it is," he remarked. "That Holmes chap has a calming influence on even the most diabolical of characters, excepting that poor misguiding fool, Professor Moriarty."

He laughed. "Poor fool lost his life when he was run over by his duplicate as he thought he was stealing to safety from one of his hideous crimes."

It was after he spoke that he noticed how quiet it was. Unusually quiet.

He neared the residences where his Midnight Angel dwelled and smiled in anticipation.

But he never made it that far.

He heard very odd footsteps behind him, sort of like what an animal with very large paws might make, or hooves, but with a slithery edge to the sound, like a snake or serpent might make.

"Say there!" He remarked, turning slowly about.

"Who's following me?"

He reached for his baton club he always took from the racks onboard the Merchant Queen, his work ship. It was large enough to crack the skull of a full-sized dragon, not that he would ever meet one, but you never knew these days with all the magical happenings going on.

But what he saw was neither snake, nor dragon.

But something else entirely different. It was a man, but not a man. It was a woman, but not a woman. It was an animal, but it did not walk like an animal.

It had claws and a barbed tail with multiple suckers at its tip instead of sharp points. Its eyes were bulbous and huge, popping out like that of a fish might. It had hands that were like curled ropes with fingers that wove in and out of each other.

Its hair was a mass of writhing worms.

Its eyes...

Its eyes were...

Death!

His scream lost to the ears of others that night.

And his Midnight Angel would miss him more than he would ever know.

Forever!

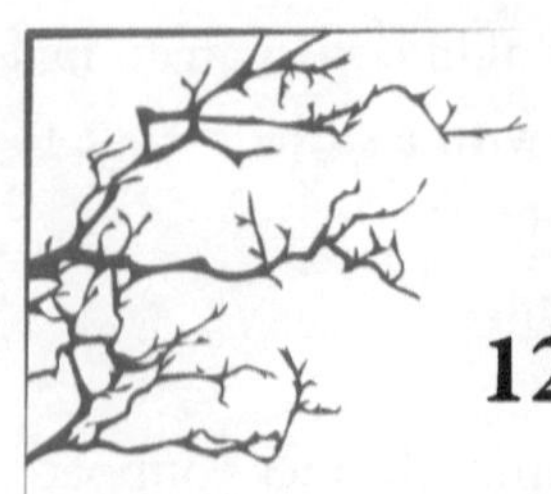

1212 Memory Lane

Harry woke with a start. His heart was pounding. So was his front door.

He hurried on a night robe, slipped into some warm slippers, then rushed to the front door.

He opened it.

"Harry, we need you," Constable Evans told him, looking apologetic and a bit at a loss for words, even though he had managed well enough.

Harry did not need to ask why. "The same?"

Constable Evans nodded.

"Holmes requested you join him immediately at your pleasure," Constable Evans told him.

Harry smiled. "A contradiction if ever I heard one, but just give me a minute to slip into some warm clothing and I'll be right with you."

He turned back to the Constable, "About my friends..."

"Already there," Constable Evans told him.

"Oh," Harry replied, a bit irked that they had beat him to the crime scene.

scotland Yard Morgue

HARRY FELT LIKE HE was blasting into the dark, dank, cold depths of the morgue as Constable Evans urged him inside. He was a bit irritated, more from lack of sleep than dealing with another death. But when he saw the somber faces of his friends, he at once felt regret for his thoughts, if not for his actions.

"Show me!" He urged Watson, who nodded and uncovered the dead body on the gurney.

Harry felt his evening meal begin to rise into his throat and looked away.

The opposing marks yet again on the throat of the victim.

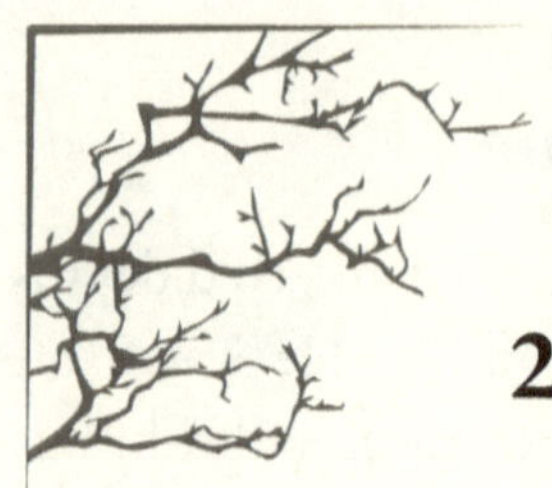

221B Baker Street

Harry stood with his hands behind his back one moment, then would reach to his side and feel for his wand the next, as if unsure it had suddenly gotten a mind of its own and decided to wander off somewhere he had no ideas as to where to find it.

It was another nightmare that drove him to wakefulness at times. He had spoken to Merlin about it and the man had told him that he was warned.

"What kind of warning?" Harry had asked him.

"To not rely on just your magic powers, but..." Merlin tapped his head, then his heart. "But to trust in these even more. For power can only do so much in the end, Harry. What makes us different from most mortal men is that we use wisdom to guide the God given powers we have honed, not anger, or hatred or lust for power."

"Harry," Holmes called him.

Harry turned about, snapping out of his memories about Merlin. *Strange how they came up so strongly at times such as this.*

Ms. Hudson had set a huge meal upon the table, and everyone was settling in for an exceedingly early breakfast with as much vigor as if they had only just arisen from their beds. But not one of them looked fresh and perky. Far from it, you could see the tell-tale signs of dark shadows under eyes, a paling of the cheeks and a cold sweat that set on from extreme exhaustion.

Harry sat next to Watson on his left and Challenger on his right.

Conan passed over a plate of biscuits to Challenger who took three, then passed the rest to Harry, who shook his head.

Challenger, then, passed the plate to Watson, who took one, passed to Holmes, who also shook his head.

Once everyone had a biscuit that wanted one, and butter and fresh marmalade, they began dishing out a fresh porridge into bowls set before them. Once all bowls were brimming with the steaming brew, they began dipping biscuits into their porridge to soak them, and then would eat small bites, or in Watson's case large bites.

Ms. Hudson finished pouring coffee for Watson, and then passed the pot around until all had coffee. Harry drank his at once in one gulp and then poured a second one.

"Harry, you'll scald your throat that way!"

Challenger warned.

Harry shook his head. "For a man who's used to eating flaming swords, hot coffee is like drinking iced tea such as what they serve in the newer refrigerated cafes."

Holmes smiled. "Suspect you would not feel it in any case, Harry, this death has struck a nerve in you."

Harry nodded. "Indeed, it has, Holmes."

"Why?"

Harry drank up his second cup and held it back out for a refill. While Conan kindly did so for him, Harry answered, "Both cases the marks were the same. Puckered like a leech might mark."

"Yes," Holmes agreed with a nod. He had already concluded after the first case but was unwilling to say more until the next one, which he was certain would happen and had, unfortunately. Much to his deep regret and the loss of those poor innocent souls.

"And the marks are not just of a leech."

Harry took his pure white napkin with beautiful red roses knit on its four corners by Ms. Hudson, who watched in fascination beside Watson as he created three mounds of fresh pepper, then covered them with white mounds of salt. He repeated the pattern in the

opposing direction.

"What's the purpose of this, Harry?" Conan asked, increasingly curious about where this was going.

"In translation theory…these opposing substances are believed to hold great power when configured a certain manner and the proper words are spoken."

Holmes nodded. "Assume you're referring to the Translation of Magic?"

"I am," Harry replied.

Harry next took out his wand and touched the three mounds on both sides. Each burst into a blue glowing mound of blue fire.

Ms. Hudson let out a surprised yelp. Harry smiled at her. "Don't worry; it won't burn your beautiful tablecloth, Ms. Hudson."

"Should hope not, or I shall have to have John here have a proper speaking to you."

Watson laughed. "I'm sure words coming from your mouth would be much more powerful than mine, my dear."

Ms. Hudson smiled. "Thank you, sweets," she replied, then gave him a scowl, when she realized why had said that.

Holmes almost cringed at the endearments, but

went on to say, "What is the purpose of this demonstration?"

Suddenly, the mounds began to pucker and as they did tiny heads began to peer from them.

Both Watson and Conan at once jumped from their chairs and backed up.

Challenger's face tightened, as he strove to understand what Harry was up to.

Holmes's face was stone. No register of emotion whatsoever as he considered the ramification of what Harry had summoned.

Harry tapped the tablecloth in front of the mounds with his magic wand and they collapsed into a flow of liquid that quickly flowed onto an empty napkin and drained into it, then vanished entirely.

Ms. Hudson looked to be close to a bout of screaming, as well as Conan and Watson.

Harry hurriedly tried to make amends for his demonstration, which he had not realized, and he should have, was so terrifying to his friends.

He plucked the napkin up and flung it into the air. It burst into flames and then a dove flew from it. It flew about the room several times, but when Harry raised a forefinger, it came to land on it.

Harry began stroking the back of the bird's neck. It rolled its eyes up in pleasure and began making sweet cooing sounds.

"Can I have it, Harry? Can I?" Ms. Hudson asked. Her terror of what she had seen had totally vanished at the sight of the lovely creature.

She loved birds even more than cooking, but John insisted they should not be kept in a cage. They should be free. So, she had not kept any, even though she loved them so much. Which is why she was keeping her kitchen window open most of the day and night, so she could hear the birds playing outside in the feeder she had made for them and bathing, then singing happily in contentment.

"Magic is a two-edged sword," Harry explained as he handed over the dove to Ms. Hudson. The bird at once hopped to her right shoulder and shoved itself into her hair next to her ear, where it ruffled up, put its head in its feathers and began a nap.

Watson eyed the creature uncertainly, but Ms. Hudson was so endeared by the creature's sweetness that when Watson started to scowl at it, she shook her head.

He got the message and caught himself. Smiling, he

raised his hands defensively. "Who am I to stand in the way of you, my dear?"

She gave him a look of relief and gratitude.

Harry continued speaking. "When used the proper way it can heal, summon beautiful things, like this wonderful dove that our dear Ms. Hudson is so kindly giving a home to now..." He looked at Watson, who rolled his eyes.

"Or...he tapped where the puckered salt and pepper had lain. "Or...it can be twisted and dark and used for torture, brutality and murder."

"Are you saying that those things we saw could have killed us?"

"Not while I'm alive of course," Harry answered with a grin. "Would never have allowed it."

Watson cleared his throat. "Then they were dangerous."

"No, they were magically warded from doing you harm. But they might have otherwise," Harry explained, realizing now that his little demonstration had gotten him into a bit of trouble.

Holmes saw the trend of thoughts and intervened on Harry's behalf. "Your point in all this, Harry, is that the two victims we've so far examined..."

"...Were not murdered by a man or woman," Harry added.

"Then what were they slain by?" Conan asked, perplexed by Harry's answer.

Harry squinted at the tip of his magic wand, as if it might suddenly leap out and attack him. He hurriedly put it back in its holster on his belt.

"Lovecraft, I assume," Holmes answered for Harry. He cocked his head to look at Harry better. "I am correct in this, am I not?"

"You are, Holmes, but how did you know that?"

Holmes reached behind him, where he had lain the book, he had been reading. He put it on the table.

Conan's eyes lit up. "You've been reading my latest novel!"

"And quite compelling I might add," Holmes replied with a nod.

Conan then saw where this was heading and almost gasped as he said, "Lovecraft is the villain of my story. Are you saying that that man is alive here and now?"

Harry and Holmes both nodded.

Harry leaned forward to see Conan's face better. "Conan, as you know from what you learned when you died on your world and transferred to this one, there are an infinite number of worlds like ours…"

Conan jumped in. "Lovecraft exists on many of them, if not all."

"Not only that," Holmes added, "But each version of Lovecraft is slightly different in appearance, as well as temperament."

Conan gave Harry and Holmes a puzzled look.

Harry shook his head. "On one of those worlds you have contacted a Lovecraft who is not just a writer of dark and evil things…"

"But also, a wizard. A very, very dark one," Holmes added. "I'm afraid, dear Conan; you have somehow managed to open up a portal to that world and brought him forth into ours."

"But to what purpose would he be coming here?" Conan demanded, not liking the direction of this discussion one bit.

"Why to find us all and kill us, of course, Conan," Holmes replied with the slightest of smiles. He had to restrain his emotions at that moment, because it brought up exceedingly powerful and disturbing memories of a loved one murdered by that fiend.

"Us. But how would he even know where and who we were?" Conan demanded.

Holmes opened Conan's book and read, "Lovecraft was a dark soul, but an extremely clever one, much more so than the fabulous Professor Moriarty who came to a fast and calamitous ending."

Holmes looked at the others a moment to give them a chance to digest the words, then he continued.

"Lovecraft was invited by Watson to his home on Baker Street, where he learned of Sherlock Holmes and his deeds."

Holmes sighed next, and then continued. "Whereas he at once felt a great loathing for the doctor and his friend. Having never known true friendship in his life, except that given to him by demons and devils, he felt it to be his mission and his honor to set out after the famous Baker Street heroes and to eliminate each one of them in as hideous and horrible a manner as possible."

Holmes paused, and then flipped through the pages momentarily to reveal an image.

"Dear God!" Conan cried out.

Harry paled.

Challenger almost gagged.

Ms. Hudson started, but Watson took her hand and clenched it securely, giving her some sense of protection.

Holmes shut the book softly. But it could have been a bomb going off for the effect it had.

Challenger set down his coffee, which he had been holding frozen in the grip of his hand as he listened. "This is simply horrible. Horrible. Conan has used the ritual that Harry just revealed to us."

Conan felt sick to his soul.

Challenger put a hand on his friend's shoulder. "Forgive yourself, Conan, how could you have known that this fantasy of yours had any merit to it. However, foul it might have been."

Conan looked even more distressed.

Ms. Hudson went to him and circled his shoulders with her arms and hugged him.

"We love you, Arthur. Do not ever doubt that."

The men watched that a moment in silence. And Conan retreated from his self-loathing as he absorbed the warmth of their concern into his soul. These were his friends, not judges of his character.

"Yes," Harry said, eying both Holmes and Conan a moment. "And now that he knows where we are, we must do everything in our power to remain alert. For death follows us as surely as the sun brings day."

"Then why these two victims," Watson demanded.

Harry looked to Holmes, who replied. "Doctor, you must spend more time reading the histories of the people you work with."

"They knew us?"

Holmes did not reply. The look in his eyes said everything Watson could need or want to know.

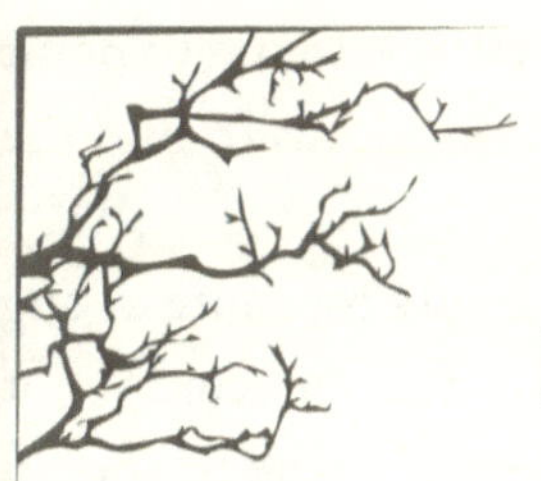

Horrors Unfold

He regretted losing the familiarity of his home; but it became important for him to become less visible now that his wife's murder was not only in the news, but in the hands of the people he hated: Scotland Yard and Holmes!

He did not know why he had such an intense hatred for all of them, but he did. And it became more heated after each murder, rather than abated and put on a backburner for another time, another place.

Instead, he found himself finding comfort in deep and dark thoughts, of unpleasant things that dwelled on the edge of time and space, waiting for a poor soul to admit them into here, so they could wreak horror and havoc.

He obliged them.

In exchange he became stronger. Lived longer. Though how he knew that he was not certain.

It was the first thing he had done once he had crossed into this new world. Renew his boundaries, and his bounds to what had come before, but which were now in this parallel world, from what he had read of in Doctor Watson's journals. Alike in ways, the worlds were, but also unlike enough, filled with enough differences of which many quite are quite subtle, others not so much. Each difference whether similar or wide, still enclosed in a like body and mind.

So, it had not been hard for him to remove the original Lovecraft. The man, who professed a love of horror, had discovered that real horror was not so pleasant.

It was to his benefit that the true Lovecraft isnever be found to point the finger at him. His first act upon entering this world was to find the author and put an end to his story.

Though why he had done so had upset him deeply for quite a long time. He remembered coming into this world; but he could not remember how or why. He only knew he was no longer where he should have been. Something had struck the memory of his past from him as he came into this dark and miserable world.

He shrugged off those confusing thoughts and focused again on his purpose now. He had to have more time to set up his headquarters before he directly attacked the famous detective and his family of friends. But he was patient. He had time. He eyed the stone at the top of his cane. It glowed briefly for a moment, as if acknowledging his awareness of it and it of him, and then dimmed again.

Yes, he had all the time in the world.

He smiled as he knocked on the door before him. He turned to eye the flat opposite his own. 221B.

Yes, he had the time and soon he would have so, so much more.

The front door opened.

He tightened his tie a bit and smiled warmly at the old man who stood there.

He gave him his card that he had prepared for this occasion.

The old man read it quickly, his eyes widening. "You're that man?"

Lovecraft smiled. "I am."

"So honored to meet you, sir. What can I do for you?"

"Would like to rent the flat you have available."

"Oh, but you can afford so much nicer than I have here," protested the old man.

Lovecraft shook his head. "Not concerned for such mortal things. How much space does it have?"

The old man eyed Lovecraft with a sharp eye. He
would like the flat. "Two bedrooms. One you could

convert into a study or what would you call it...?"

"Writing den," Lovecraft offered.

"Yes, yes, that," the Old Man replied. "And you will have no need for a kitchen; I and my wife supply all meals. It is in the rental."

"And does it have a view of the street?"

The Old Man hesitated for a moment, thinking this might be a deal breaker. Not many renters liked to hear traffic all day and night, even if the nights were quieter. Lately with the increasing numbers moving into London, the traffic was becoming larger and larger.

"A masterful one."

He looked up.

Lovecraft spotted the window at once. It was what he thought. What he had seen!

"Take it!"

Lovecraft did not wait to see whether the Old Man would accept or not, he stepped inside at once and headed for the stairs.

The Old Man shrugged and shut the door.

If only he had known it was not the Lovecraft, whose works he admired and loved, but a far darker and more sinister one, he might have been more reluctant to rent to this gentleman.

But he did not.

And he did.

"Such is the fate of fools and wise men, that what is written in the stars is not so easily seen on one's own forehead."

—Doctor John Watson

The Mansion of Lovecraft

Harry, Challenger, and Conan stood at the entrance of one of the grander buildings of older London. Just off Wilkerson and Hyde, it stood a good three stories tall with gabled roofs, and multiple chimneys spewing smoke into the morning skies.

Tall Elder trees fronted the building, and a plethora of flowering gardens rousted the front fence all the way to the front porch, where they played like sweet friends of an assortment of colors of gold, red and amber along the front boards of the porch.

Bushy and fragrant evergreens, stunted in their growth deliberately, interspersed between the various flower gardens.

The pungent and sweet cloying smells of flowers and greens were so aromatic that poor Conan was beginning to feel his throat, sinuses and eyes swell up.

He sneezed. Not once, but over and over.

"What's come over you, Conan?" Challenger asked, worried for his friend.

Conan shook his head. "Do not worry, Challenger, it is not an illness. I merely react to such strong scents."

"Have you asked Doctor Watson to address this?"

Harry asked, equally as concerned.

"I have not. Nor will I. Need I remind you that I am a doctor as well?"

Harry touched his friend's shoulder and squeezed it warmly. "No, you do not."

He turned back to the front door and took hold of the large knocker upon it. It felt odd in the palm of his hand, as the knocker was carved to appear like one of the fabled monsters from the darkest of hells, with long tusks, blazing red eyes and hair that hung down the brisk wood paneling of the door.

Challenger noted the look. "Only a writer..."

"Or a performer," Conan added.

"...Would do such a miserable thing to their home," Challenger finished, giving Conan a warm smile and a nod of thanks.

After several loud and voluminous pounds on the door seemed to cause the home to tremble for several moments the door finally opened.

But only after a tiny hole opened in another gargoyle like figure high above the knocker. A single bloodshot eye peered out a long moment, roamed over their bodies, then the hole shut with a bang.

As the door opened a tall skeletal figure stepped to

block their way further. He had hair as equally long as the door knockers and eyes just as ruby red, though they were bloodshot.

"Can't a vampire get a moment's quiet to sleep anymore?" He demanded.

Challenger spoke up first. "We are here to speak with Mister Lovecraft."

The vampire smiled, revealing two huge yellowed canine teeth that dripping blood.

"Ah, the man who sold his house to me."

"Sold his house?" Harry asked. "But that is impossible. He would never sell his grandfather's ancestral home."

"To a vampire?" The vampire asked with a sardonic smile on his lips.

"No, to anyone. And I will have you know that one of my best friends is a vampire."

The vampire shook his head. "Not likely. Most mortals shun us. And friends? Never!"

Conan did a most uncharacteristic thing for himself. He shoved his face into that of the vampires and said, as he tilted his face up and stood on his tip toes to get close enough, "Sir! You insult my friend's honor and ours. Count Dracula is our friend. All of ours!"

The vampire stood there a moment, its smile vanquished by Conan's statement and then he stepped back and gestured them inside. "Be welcome then. But I warn you, be careful of my pet."

As they entered a huge werewolf looking creature, lashed to a post leaped towards them, causing Conan to pee his pants.

The vampire shut the door.

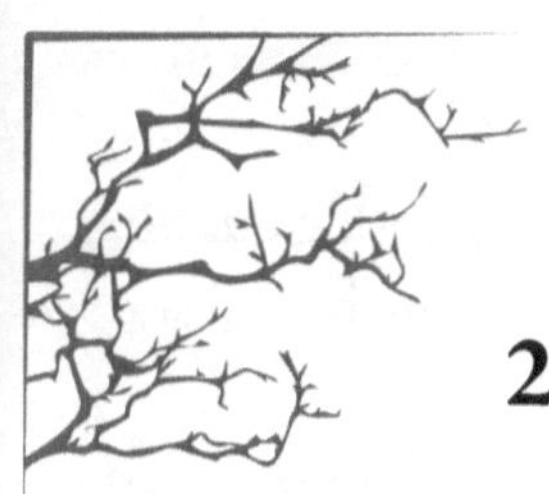

221B Baker Street

Ms. Hudson hurried to the front door, upon which a fist was pounding vigorously. She opened it. Constable Evans stood there, an apologetic expression on his face.

"I'm sorry, Ms. Hudson, for breaking your rest, but we have need of Holmes and Watson immediately."

The clamor of footsteps coming down the stairs and Holmes, shrugging on his coat, and Watson yawning big, then pulling his own on, joined them.

"We heard you pull up, Constable," Holmes told him when he looked surprised.

Watson turned to Holmes and shifted his black medical bag from his left hand to his right. "You heard him drive up. You never sleep! I, however," he yawned again. "...Am in much need of my beauty sleep."

Ms. Hudson gave him a side hug. "Oh, John, don't be such a grumbly bear!"

She ducked back into her flat, and then came out with a cloth bag from which heavenly odors rose to tease Watson's nostrils.

"How?" He asked.

She smiled.

Holmes nodded to her and followed Constable Evans out.

Watson gave Ms. Hudson a sweet kiss and he would have given her a hug as well, but he had his medical bag in his right hand and the cloth bag of fresh baked scones in the other.

"Sorry, must hurry, Martha. The game's afoot!" He told her and scrambled down the porch to join his friends as they climbed into Constable Evans police wagon.

She waved as they drove off and then shook her head. "Is there ever a time when the game is not?"

Unseen by her, a man is watching her from the opposing building.

As if she somehow sensed him, she quickly looks up, but all she sees is the movement of curtains and nothing more.

She waits a moment, then reenters the building and shuts the door.

"Must be the wind building up for another blustery day," she told herself, though not believing a word of what she said.

She could not shake the undeniable feeling that something horrible was about to happen. Something

from her nightmares.

She shut the door to her flat and went back to the kitchen. She examined the huge pile of dishes and cooking utensils. "A woman's job is never done," she sighed, but then she quickly got back into her happy mood once more and began cleaning up.

Worry about what you can change, not what you cannot, she told herself as she prepared for a new day that more than likely would be longer than usual...as usual! She smiled to herself.

JOURNEY OF MAGIC

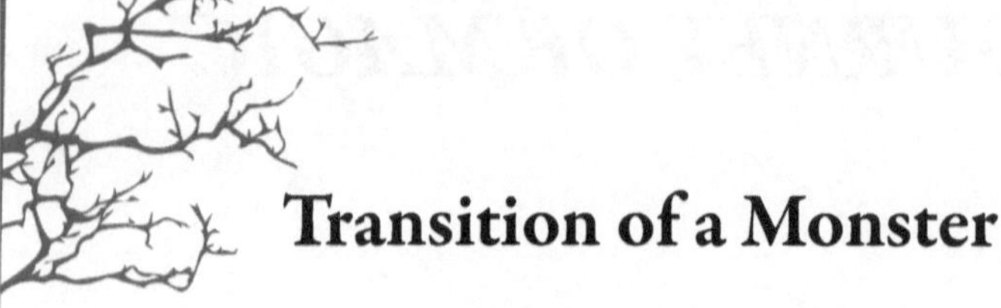

Transition of a Monster

The alley was cordoned off by Scotland Yard, with constables at both ends of it. But somehow, he managed to slip past them anyway. He was invisible to them, or more likely they were bored and not paying attention to the old man picking his nose, coughing, and staggering as if he were drunk.

The constables were hardened to the sight of such rabble that they barely noticed them after a while. Those sorts usually were only problems in the sense that they smelled awful, had atrocious manners and were homeless.

The homeless were not looked down upon by them, merely seen as part of the scenery of modern London. Even with the good Queen Mary of Scots intentions to make sure that there were no further homeless, it was impossible for her to help them all. There were just too many. The wealth of the country was concentrated into too few hands to spread the wealth any further without crippling the government's resources.

The old man, once past the somewhat lax constables, suddenly straightened up, took longer strides, his finger from his nose and dropped to a knee further into the rubble. Once so, he took out magnifying glass and peered closely at the oddly colored rubble set before him.

It had been part of the magical pentagram on the right side and had fallen apart, the wall that is, but not the occult symbol. It remained intact, but smaller somehow, as if the very wall itself had caused it to expand and spread its deadly arms.

"Curious," the old man mumbled in a familiar voice. That of Sherlock Holmes.

A sound just ahead of him alerted him. He looked up and saw something slithering through the rubble towards him. As it made its way closer it appeared to be growing larger and larger, until as it neared him it had grown to the size of a small elephant in height, but with sides that stretched a good several yards in either direction, and a hump with fins that were sprouting upwards as it stopped and began to rise before Holmes.

Its blank face sprouted eyes, which opened and glared at Holmes.

"Most curious," Holmes said, slowly rising from his kneeling position. He slowly put away his magnifying glass, but as he did so he noticed that the pentagram at his foot was beginning to grow.

A sour hissing sound alerted him to further movement from the gigantic monster that was now towering a good ten feet above his head.

The constables had finally noticed him, but in doing so, they also saw the creature about to attack him.

They became immobilized with fear.

Holmes was not.

He turned on his heels to run away from the monster.

It struck at him the same time as the pentagram spread out waves of violet energy. The waves thinned into tentacles and wrapped about the feet of Holmes, collapsing him to the rough and tumble rubble about him.

He tried to break free, but his legs would not move. As he struggled, his cape was torn from his back, and his cap fell off, mingling with the debris.

He managed to twist about just as the monster opened a mouth as large as a small carriage and lunged for him.

The constables broke free from their fear and rushed to aid the old man. But the monster swallowed the old man the same time as the pentagram sent out a blast of searing energy which flung them from their feet.

She

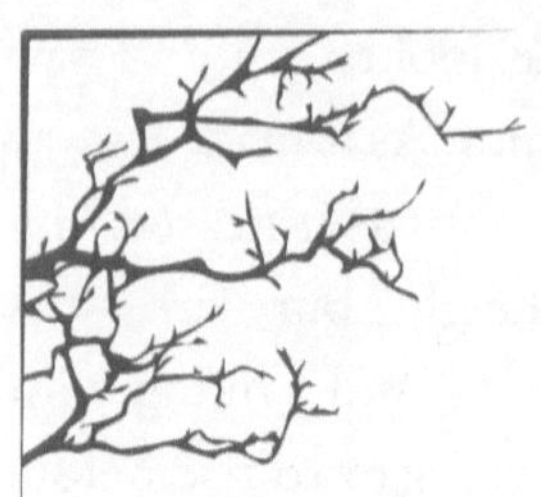

Her dark form twisted in anger from her vantage point above the alley floor. Her eyes flashed with demonic fury. "No!" She cursed.

The Baron stepped through a shadow near her and put a hand on her shoulder. "You failed."

"Only because you sent that monster after him the same time as I struck!" she told him, turning her face to him.

"We're merely players in a larger game, dear one."

Then, even as his face smiled and turned into that of a beautiful woman, who sneered, he backed into the shadows and vanished.

She turned back again to look at the debris below, her eyes still burning with fury, her hands curling into angry fists.

That Baron, she thought, a leader of fools. And I am one of them! She thought bitterly.

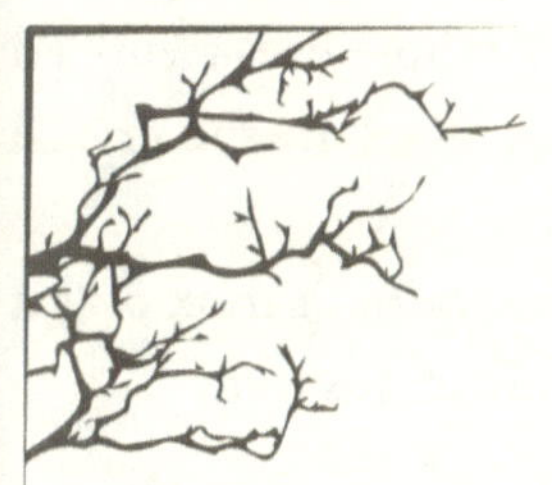

Premonition

Harry had nodded off next to the fire in his sitting room. Challenger laid akimbo the large couch and Conan spread out on the largish settee with its comfortable velvet cushions.

Ms. Hudson was nowhere seen, but her voice, humming cheerfully, could be heard in the nearby kitchen.

Harry's crystal ball on the table laid motionless and dark, but suddenly a blast of light shot forth from it, lighting up the entire room.

Harry woke first.

He jumped up from his chair to get to the table before the light dimmed.

Challenger and Conan were so startled that it took them several moments to remember where they were. They climbed to their feet and rushed to look as well.

"What was that, Harry?" Ms. Hudson hollered from the kitchen. She came running into the room, a loaf of French bread in one hand and a knife in the other. "It felt like someone had turned up the heater."

"We don't have a heater," Harry told her.

"Know, silly!" She told him, and then saw where he was. "Oh! That explains it then."

Harry gave her a piercing stare for a moment, and then looked back to crystal ball where a tiny, but familiar figure was forming.

Ms. Hudson reached the table and peered between Conan and Challenger.

Watson, who Harry had sent to his own bedroom to rest, stumbled into the room, wiping at his eyes. "What in God's name caused my room to heat up so much?"

Harry looked at him and then at Ms. Hudson, whose eyes twinkled mischievously, but said nothing. He turned again, back to the crystal ball.

Watson, however, paused at the entrance to the room. It took only a glance for him to figure out what had startled him from his rest.

"What is it, Harry? What do you see?"

Harry gave Watson a smile.

Watson rushed over to look as well. "Oh dear," he muttered.

The Lost and Found

Inspector Bloodstone and Constable Evans approached Harry's front door. Constable Evans took the huge golden knocker shaped like a Medusa's head and slammed it home against the varnished wood of the door.

A hammering sound thumped inside and outside.

Several moments passed, and then the door opened.

Ms. Hudson gestured to them to enter.

"Ms. Hudson, why are you here?" The Inspector demanded, surprised at her appearance.

"Harry will explain," she told them, but said no more.

They entered the hallway before them and she led them to the sitting room, where the crystal ball was now draped with a thick black velvet cloth. Harry finished scooting it to the middle of the table and then turned to greet his visitors.

"Inspector. Constable," he greeted. "So good of you to come."

The Inspector glanced about the room. "This is where you hold your séances."

"Question or fact, Inspector?" Harry quipped.

The Inspector brushed off the question and sat down at the table glaring at the covered crystal ball as if it might at any moment leap up and attack him.

Constable Evans gave Harry a tiny shake of his head and Harry's eyebrows arched, but he said nothing.

Harry turned to look as Ms. Hudson came back into the room.

The Inspector had not realized she left until she returned with a pot of steaming coffee and a small tray of biscuits and jam.

"I'm sure you're both famished," she said.

Constable Evans eyed the biscuits. "We did rush from home when we got the message."

"Good, then I'm sure your father won't mind you eating something. You're a growing young man, after all."

The Inspector made a face. "What happened? I was led to believe by Challenger and Conan that you had discovered something important."

Harry nodded. "We did. But..." He hesitated to speak further.

The Inspector was about to pour some coffee and hesitated. He turned to look at Harry. "Well, what did you see? Busy man. No time for charades or musical

chairs!"

Harry glanced at Ms. Hudson. She nodded.

"Well, yes and no."

The Inspector finished pouring himself coffee, and then did the same for his son, who scooted the plate of biscuits to his father.

"How can there be two different things then?" The Inspector asked, truly puzzled at the response he had been given. "It's either you saw something you need to tell me...NOW..." He emphasized, "...Or you have merely diverted me to a lovely snack thanks to our very lovely, Ms. Hudson."

He felt like a sponge that had been squeezed too many times this morning. He had lost a lot of sleep when he heard that Holmes had died. And now his worry and frustration were surfacing big time. He did not like all these mind games the fellowship of Holmes played at times.

But then he frowned. *Course, I am part of it too*, he realized in his mind. He shrugged.

Even though such things had happened before, each time it happened again, he felt traumatized. He had a lot of respect for the detective, and he had to admit, though he never would say that in public, that he saw him as a

second son of sorts.

"Speak up, I haven't all morning, you know!"

He glanced at Constable Evans, feeling momentarily guilty over those feelings, then back to Harry. "Explain."

Harry sighed. He toyed with his own cup of coffee a moment, and then said. "You'll understand better once I show you."

Harry reached across the table and pulled the cloth away from the crystal ball.

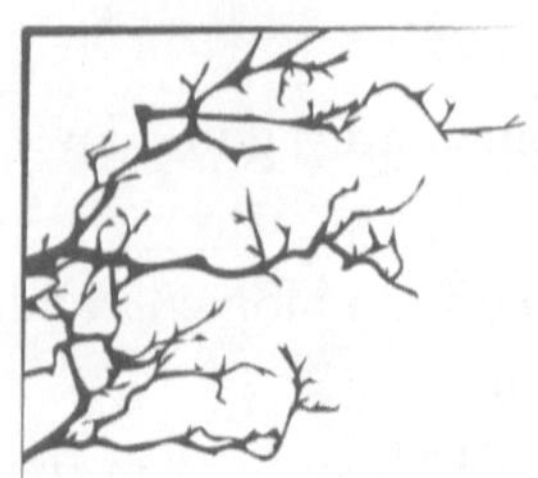

Scatter World

Holmes lay stunned on the green meadow he had fallen upon in the explosion of magic and monsters he had experienced. One moment he was laying in the rubble of the occult explosion of the alley and swallowed by a monstrous creature, and then he found himself tumbling end over end, arms and legs flailing for something solid and then he was flung hard against this surface.

He had lain there stunned a long time, even though he had been lucky enough to fall into a bank of moss and flowers.

But more luckily for him, his reflexes were fast, and he had managed to soften his landing by curling up into a ball before he struck, lessening the force of the impact to his back and head.

But it had still been hard.

Whatever had struck him from his world into wherever he was now had been powerful and brutal. It was raw magic. Powerful and brutish. Unlike any magic he had experienced before.

He did not try to move at first. He wanted to assess his body first to make sure nothing was broken. But all his limbs and extremities were able to move without any great pain. Except for the bruising he had received from the tumble he was in remarkably decent shape, if still a bit winded.

He saw a beautifully cloudless sky above him and trees the size of small mountains that clasped at the oddly colored sun overhead. Or was it suns? He noticed that the shadows falling across the tree trunks and ground were not the same color and there were more than one.

Also, peering down from the lowest of the branches were the most beautiful birds he had ever seen.

They sat on the lowest branches, which were about twenty feet off the ground and as thick as an elephant's girth. Their plumage was all shades of the rainbow and many of them had very human like faces but covered with feathers of radiant color. They were noticeably quiet, watching him, as if weighing whether he was a threat or not.

Finally, they began talking to each other again, as if having decided and started ruffling up, preening their feathers, and chirping to each other, much as ordinary birds do.

Finally, he felt strong enough to sit up. He did so.

Dizzy a moment, he waited a bit longer, then slowly pushed himself to his feet. He swayed a moment, as if still dizzy, but then realized it was only that he was standing on a slope and that made for awkward standing.

He quickly took off the make-up he had worn to throw off Harry, Challenger, and Conan. He had done so for reasons he was surprised even now that he had followed, considering his logical nature.

The trap in the alley had been set for him or Watson and so he had triggered it, but not with his body, but with a manikin he had found in a nearby store and draped with his clothing. But he had not expected losing his real cape and cap as well at the last moment.

It had been necessary to draw out the criminals responsible for the trap that would have killed him or Watson, if not for Harry's warning.

He was proud of Harry. He might become a great detective someday. Especially, if he could ever stop relying so much on his magic to get him out of scrapes. That tended to weaken a man's intellect, to always have a tool to use when the mind is much sharper, much craftier to use.

But he had found out what he wanted to know, only

thing was how did he manage to get back to disclose it?

He began trudging through the huge forest, wary of creatures that could be overhead and out of sight that might launch upon him. The place reminded him so much of another world, a realm of great beauty and wonder.

For a moment he was lost as to where such a place might be and felt a twinge of loneliness and maybe even fear that he would never see his good friends again. But then like lightning in a cloudy sky, his mind lit up with the proper deductions. The birds. The trees. The double shadows.

He smiled.

He now knew exactly where he was!

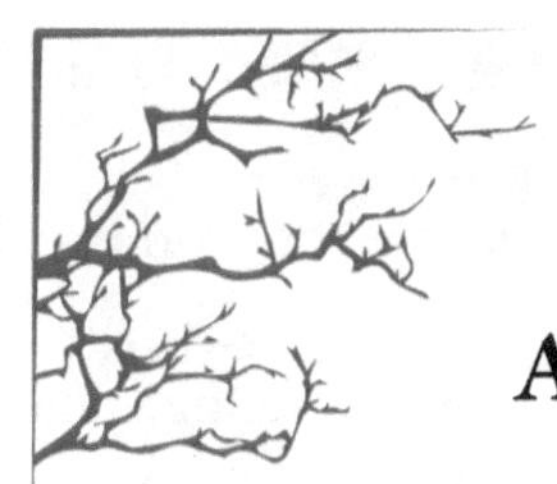

A Thousand Miles

"No, it was Lao Tse who said it!" Challenger insisted.

Conan stood up and wagged an indignant finger at his friend.

"It was Confucius!"

"No," Challenger roared, his face growing red with anger. "It was not!"

Conan stepped closer to Challenger, as if he might punch him in the face, his hands curling into fists. "Are you saying I'm an idiot then?"

Challenger sneered. "An idiot does as an idiot says!" He spoke.

Conan stepped closer still, his face redder than before. "You are saying I'm an idiot then!"

"Not then, but now!" Challenger finished.

Conan raised a hand to take a swing at Challenger and it struck the side of a tray held in Ms. Hudson's hands.

She expertly juggled the tray and its contents to stop from spilling them, and then gave Conan and Challenger a scowl.

"Shut up and sit down!" Ms. Hudson yelled at the two men as she rebalanced her large tray of sandwiches and a pot of coffee.

They both quickly sat down, even more red-faced than before. Ashamed of how they had acted in front of the very lovely and kind, Ms. Hudson. But neither willing to apologize.

Ms. Hudson sighed. "Between Holmes being gone; and that dreary trip to America, I'm thinking we are all in need of a long, long vacation."

"I'm not," Challenger said, staring at Conan as if daring him to disagree.

Conan lifted his chin up stubbornly. "Nor I. I feel perfectly fit and fine."

"Ever since you came back from that trip to America, you two have been at each other's throats!" She pointed out.

"Either say what's bothering you or stop the stupid bickering!" She warned them, wagging her own finger then. But at both.

Challenger crossed his arms.

Conan crossed his.

Neither looked at the other.

Harry entered from below with Watson. They mentioned silverware and a huge platter of scones with a cup of butter and honey upon it.

"Dinner is served!" Watson pointed out happily.

"For you maybe," Challenger growled.

"I'm not hungry. Now!" Conan spit out for emphasis.

Ms. Hudson stepped between the two men and took an ear of both and pulled it upwards.

"Ow!" Challenger roared.

"Ow!" Howled Conan.

She looked them both in their faces, her own red with anger. "Will not tolerate such boyishness from either of you and not in this house, you understand me?"

"But it's not your house!" Protested Challenger.

"He's right," Agreed Conan.

She tugged harder on their ears.

"I said stop it!"

Neither spoke up.

She pulled harder.

"I asked you a question!" She exclaimed, demanding they speak up as she asked.

Both men cried out in pain and nodded their heads. She let go and left them, heading back downstairs.

"Men!" She uttered in disgust.

Watson broke into laughter.

Ms. Hudson hollered up the stairs, "Don't make me come back up there, John."

Watson shut up.

All three men eyed each other like a classroom of boys scolded by their teacher.

Harry sighed and sat down. He scooped several sandwiches onto a plate, several scones, and then began buttering them and adding honey.

"I think it's the stress of not knowing that is getting to us," Harry pointed out.

Challenger eyed him sternly. "You showed him to us in your crystal ball. You said you knew he was alive and where!"

"I merely said I knew he was alive. I did not say I know exactly where he is, only that I know where he is."

Watson scowled at Harry. "Harry that makes absolutely no sense whatsoever," he argued as he sat down next to Harry, grabbed four scones, and began buttering them and adding honey.

"Agree," Conan joined in, coming to the table and helping himself to a cup of coffee and one sandwich, which he nibbled on in tiny bites.

Challenger finally sighed and joined them. "So then where is he...generally speaking?"

Harry turned to Challenger. "Very well then, this is where I believe him to be."

The High Tea Society

The Countess and the Baron stood in front of a rundown looking restaurant and grimaced.

Other members peered through the windows, making faces, and grimacing as well.

"It's got no furniture?" A young woman asked, her face heavy with magical stripes on her right cheek.

"How are we supposed to have tea with no furniture?"

The Baron sighed. "Problems, problems, problems. Be patient. We escaped the madness that is America now, so be glad of that."

The young woman whined, "I liked San Francisco. I had lots of men to play with there."

"You don't need men, you have us!" The Baron insisted.

"That's right, Dearie," the countess added. "We are splendid company."

"You two are impossible!" The young woman complained but shut up.

The countess turned to the Baron. "Easy for you to say, she doesn't need men. You do not need men or women, since you are both! And thus, more powerful

than any of the rest of us alone."

The Baron's male face turned feminine, and his silk shirt bulged outwards as he grew breasts. His lips became pink with lipstick and his eyes heavy with liner.

"Dear Countess, there's magic and then...there's magic."

And without further word the Baron walked through the closed door, not leaving a single mark on its exterior as he passed.

The countess turned to her friends. "He's such a showoff!"

"Yes, he is," Spin said, adjusting her bifocals. Her golden hair spun above her head in a tiny tornado of energies and her amber eyes spun in pools of gold and brown as she looked at the countess.

"Ever since he lured Holmes into that trap with that false one," the countess commented. "Ever since then he has been intolerable. I worry about out little group."

Mage, who liked to be called Cheryl when she was in a good mood, or Spin when she was playful, stuck a finger in her right ear and plucked out a gold coin. She bit it, frowned, and flipped it into the air where it spun for a moment and then vanished.

"Yes, she is!" Mage told the countess, then put a

hand on the glass and it bulged inwards forming a door. She opened it and went inside. Then she looked back out. "He's not going to be stuck there for long you know. That man has nine lives like a cat!"

"What man, Dearie?" The countess asked.

Spin grinned. "The detective with the curly hair and the cute brown eyes, or where they blue? No matter. Anyway, he has been killed once by Moriarty already and that other man, what was his name?"

A man, who had been standing in the back, silent to this point in time, raised a red gloved hand and shook it at Spin. "What does it matter? It all adds up to the same, he keeps coming back!"

"He's right you know," Spin said with a grin, and then went into the restaurant.

Red Glove, as he was called by his peers, shrugged his shoulders at the countess to acknowledge it did not really matter at all, and then followed Spin inside.

The countess shook her head. "Has it come to this then that we are merely a class of rowdy students clamoring for attention?"

She tossed a hanky at the door, and it flung itself open and then bowed to her as she entered, shaking her head over and over to show her dismay.

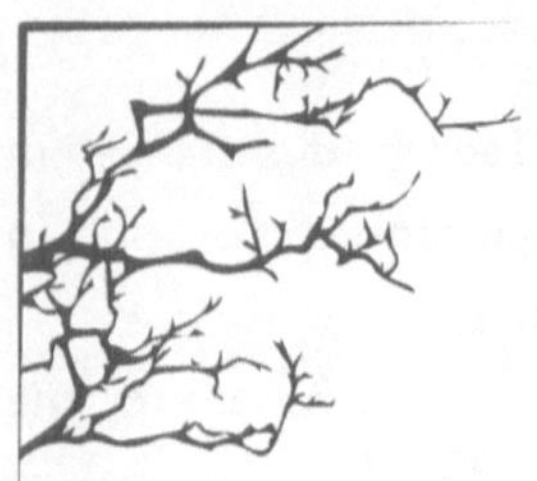

The Journey

Holmes felt so free that he wondered if he really wanted to return. It reminded him so much of Pahalgam and the splendid time he spent there in his earlier days. But here it was so much less tame, wilder. You could even taste the magic in the air.

Strands of it hung from the trees and glided through the air like clouds, spattering shrubbery and ground beneath it and causing magical things to sprout up, grow limbs, then go hopping, skipping, leaping, or running off on two, three and even four legs in a variety of shapes.

He even saw a baby dragon flapping overhead, followed closely by its parents, who gave him a stern look, but seeing no clear danger, continued after their sibling.

He continued through the forest, allowing his worries to fly away. Time enough to be concerned about the plot that had flung him here once he was safely returned to London. He found an open space and continued onto it, his mind lost in thought and that is when he met with an unexpected visitor.

As he took a turn about a huge boulder a huge dark shadow fell across him. A bestial cry erupted, causing the very ground beneath his feet to shake.

He looked for somewhere to hide, but there was none; he had gone too far into the opening.

He ran for the nearest trees, but the shadow followed him, not only followed, but grew larger and larger.

Then something fell from the sky and plucked him off the ground, just yards before he would have reached safety.

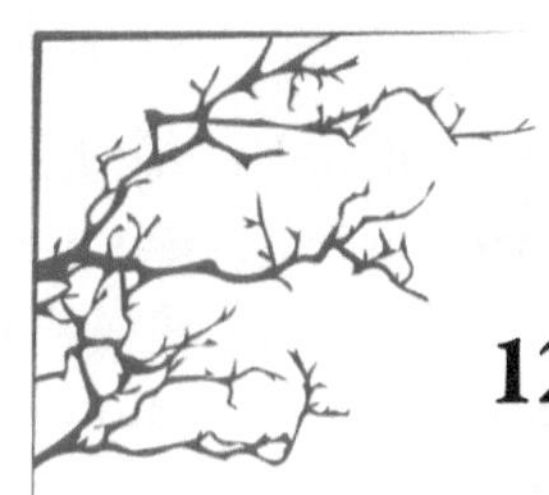

1212 Memory Lane

Challenger paced the room in a manner that caused Watson to smile, despite the constant nag of worry in the background of his mind over Holmes. He knew he was alive but knowing it and experiencing it were not the same time.

The people behind the occult trap still had not been found and that worried him. Because if he could not put a name to them, there was always the chance of Holmes still being in danger. And his friends. It was not like Watson to worry over himself. He was not that way. Being a doctor, he always thought of others first. It was why he had become a doctor in the first place, to serve others. To heal and make them well.

Now he could not even heal himself.

He growled angrily at his sense of helplessness. Then he decided.

"I'm tired of sitting around and waiting for something to happen," Watson declared.

He rose and went to the coat rack. "I, for one, am also tired of always being on the defensive in this magical war that seems to be going on forever. If not one villain, then another!" He exclaimed.

Challenger stomped a foot so hard on the floor that it shook. "Ah-ha! "He shouted.

Harry, who had been napping on his favorite chair, snapped awake, his right hand producing blue fire to defend him.

Conan, who had been eating a scone, bit his tongue instead and yelped in anger. "Drat it all! Challenger! You've made me bite my tongue."

Challenger laughed. "At least I now know of one way to get you to bite your tongue!"

Conan scowled at him. "Not funny!"

Everyone looked at Challenger, their faces surprised and angry. He finally took a deep breath and sighed. "I'm sorry. I'm just as worried as the rest of you."

"Please accept my apologies, Conan. You are my friend. You know I would never mean you harm intentionally."

Conan nodded in response to the conciliatory tone of Challenger.

Challenger sighed again. "I'm sorry, my friends, but this is indeed bigger than the lot of us. And we have been ignoring the tell-tale signs of why that is ever since we returned from America and dealt with that dreadful Mister Blaine and his demonic Hollow Hand. We still fear their hand in this evil that has befallen Holmes. We still feel they are not dead and vanquished to the pits of hell they came from."

Conan dabbed a napkin to his lips, then said, "I feel sorry for saying this, but I wish to God they were!"

"Here, here!" Watson joined in.

But Harry did not join in. He went to the table and sat down. He unclothed the crystal ball that sat there. They had retreated from 221B because the presence of Holmes overshadowed them too heavily when they were there.

None of them wanted to say it, but even with Harry's determination of where Holmes had vanished to, they still worried that it might not be true after all and that they had found the remains of a dead Holmes.

Not one of them would say so, but they still feared dreadfully for the man's life. Such good friends are hard to find and these four were certainly four of the best any man could ever want. At least that is what Harry thought as he hovered over his crystal ball. He was determined not to let Holmes down. Or his fellowship of friends.

At that moment, many things that had been

troubling him in the back of his mind and were threatening to overwhelm him became clear. He had what Holmes called an "Ah-ha!" moment.

"Ah-ha!" Harry declared.

All looked to him.

"See it clearly now," Harry explained.

"First," Harry said as the others gathered about him to watch him work.

He looked at Conan first and smiled. "When a doctor prescribes the incorrect medicine, what does he do after he realizes so?"

Conan did not have to think of the answer. It was obvious. "Examine the original diagnose for flaws."

"Exactly!" Harry exclaimed.

He then looked at Challenger, "Second, when a person explores the unknown, searching for evidence of treasure and antiquities, what should one's motto be?"

Challenger's face screwed up in thought. He was tempted to say fame and fortune, but he reconsidered that thought at once and instead answered, "Trace the roots of the rumors, of the facts, of the trail that one pursues. Look for the origins of that trail to the best of one's ability."

"Exactly!" Harry exclaimed yet again. "And once

having examined the roots, what next? What should one do then?"

"I know what I would do," Watson declared. "I would have a spot of tea and a scone."

Everyone burst into laughter, but Harry, who scowled at Watson.

"Third! Watson, I need you to think this through, I am not playing here!"

Watson, feeling more contrite, expounded, "I would very carefully work my way from the root of the facts, examining each step of the path carefully until I had ascertained where it all led."

Harry stood and offered his hand to Watson. "Exactly, Watson, and now we know what we all should do...together!"

The men all gave Harry a questioning look. Harry was quiet.

"But what about the crystal ball, Harry? You said you had seen where Holmes was sent, where he was," Challenger insisted.

"Yes," agreed Conan.

"That's right," Watson joined in.

"That's my whole point and..."

He paused a long moment to give himself the clarity

he needed to finish his argument and them a chance to digest where he was leading their thoughts.

"Fourth, the facts we have been pursuing so far have led us to where?"

The room was quiet.

Watson started to grin, a joke on his lips, and then stopped.

Harry looked around. "Holmes said that when one depends only on magic to solve one's issues, one becomes addicted to and limited by its powers. That is nothing short of self-suicide."

Challenger waved a hand in disagreement. "But Harry, your magic has never steered us wrong before."

Harry smashed a palm flat on the table, causing the crystal ball to fly off its mount and roll towards the end of the table where no one stood.

"I'll get it," Watson shouted and hurried to stop it.

"Let it fall!" Harry commanded.

Watson gave Harry a blank look and watched the crystal ball fall off the table. He winced at the thought of all that broken glass, but as he and the others waited for the sound of breaking glass, none came.

Harry gave them a triumphant smile as they crowded around the end of the table, their eyes wide with amazement at the crystal ball, which now hovered in the air, but inches from the floor.

"That which is constructed by man with magic," Harry explained. "Can also be deconstructed by magic, by man!"

Watson got it first. "Good Lord! Someone has been watching everything we do through that thing!"

Suddenly, the crystal ball began to grow larger and brighter, as a fuse had been lit.

"Everyone back!" Harry shouted.

An explosive force shattered the room with violent energies.

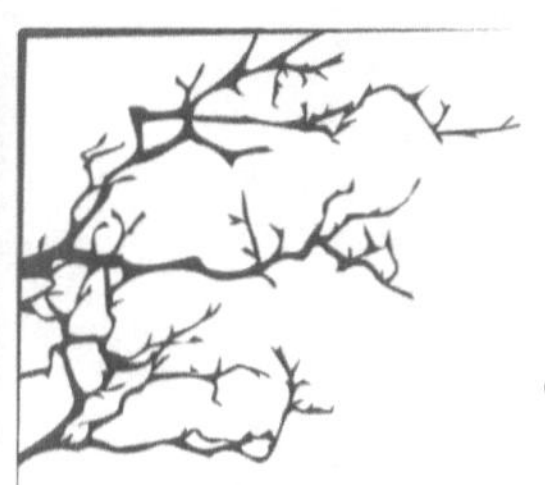

Shadow Bringer

Shadow Bringer watched from below 1212 Memory Lane on the sidewalk opposite the building. She smiled when a brilliant flash of light erupted in the room above and then the windows all exploded outwards in shards of fire, broken glass, steel, and wood.

She quickly walked into the shadows of the alley two paces away and as she did so, she vanished, as if she had never been there.

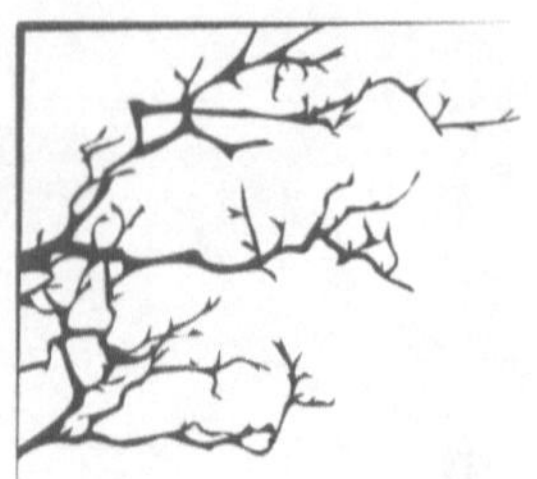

Holmes

Holmes reached his hand out and clasped that of Lord Graystone. The tall, muscular dragon lord smiled.

"Must say that dragon riding is a bit rougher than I anticipated," Holmes said.

Lord Graystone grinned. "You get used to it. Their scales are a bit rough on the inside of the things and the buttocks, but a bit of salve and time heals that."

"I'm sure," Holmes replied.

"You gave me quite a scare at first when your dragon called out," Holmes said.

Lady Shareen, seated in the limo, laughed.

Holmes looked to her.

"That was not the dragon, Sherlock. It was the love of my life here who called out."

Holmes gave Lord Graystone a surprised look.

Lord Graystone laughed. "I'm sorry, Holmes, I couldn't help myself. If you hadn't been running in the open, I would never have been able to catch you up as I did."

They stood outside 221B, a large Tesla limousine, a Ford Jaguarine, stood humming near the curb. Lady Shareen leaned forward and gave Holmes a peck on his right cheek as Lord Graystone took Holmes's hand to shake it.

"God keep you safe, Sherlock," she told him.

He grinned at her. "He has." He nodded to Lord Graystone who shrugged, let go of Holmes hand and then guided Lady Shareen into the back of the limo as he opened its door and squeezed his massive, bronzed shoulders and upper torso in to sit beside her.

He looked back at Holmes. "If you need our help again?"

Holmes smiled. "I think one dragon ride in this lifetime is quite enough, thank you!"

Lady Shareen tittered, her eyes bright with amusement. "Promise next time it won't be a dragon."

"From what you told us of that dastardly Mister Blaine, I would not rule out anything, Holmes."

"I shan't," Holmes replied.

He touched his cap.

Lord Graystone nodded goodbye and shut the door of the limo. It drove off, making a gentle humming sound that gradually grew louder as it moved away from the curb.

Holmes turned about and looked at 221B.

"Home," he said with a sigh.

He went to the front door to unlock it, but before he could fully open it, someone shrieked and then attacked him, squeezing him so hard he thought he was going to die.

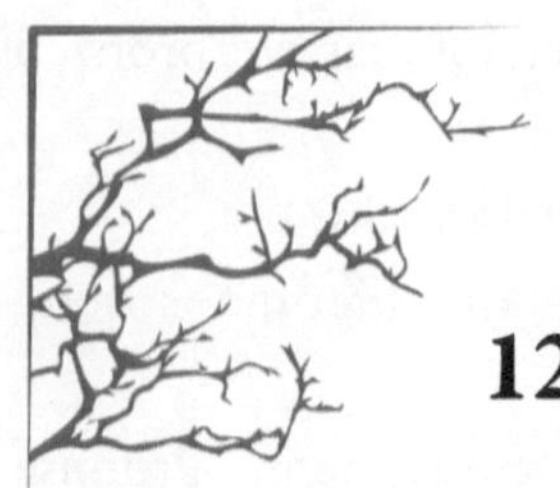

1212 Memory Lane

The four men coughed as the smoke of the still smoldering pieces of table drifted about the room. The sitting room was a shambles. The curtains were scorched by the blast, wallpaper blackened, floor littered with shards of glass, and wood.

Harry was the worst. His jacket was in tatters and smoldering. He hurriedly slapped those parts with a blazing blue hand and the smoldering stopped, but the damage had been done. He had bruises all over his body from the impact of the exploding table, but without its barrier, he and the others would surely have all perished.

Watson gazed at the broken plate on the floor and the scattered sweet rolls on the floor. He sighed sadly. "Who would have thought?"

"Indeed," Challenger agreed as he rose from the floor, brushing off debris.

Conan moaned to his left.

"Conan!"

Challenger rushed over and gave his friend a hand. "Are you all, right? Anything broken?"

"Only my pride," Conan admitted. He took a couple steps. "And my shorts seem to have caught the wrong way."

He turned about and adjusted his pants and then felt relieved.

The others broke into laughter.

Conan blushed with embarrassment and turned to face them. "That's not very sporting of you!"

Challenger shook his head, his eyes still gleaming with mirth. "Sorry, my friend, but I hardly think that pressed genitals qualify as something broken."

Conan sniffed angrily. "Maybe not for you! You have none!"

Challenger roared with even more laughter and then stopped suddenly. "What? What did you just say?"

Conan raised his fists, fearing Challenger was about to strike him.

Challenger slapped Conan on his back. "Jesting, my friend. Merely jesting. I'm happy you are fine."

He turned to the others. "Watson?"

"I'm fine." He felt his face and a cut that was bleeding there. He had bruises on the side exposed to the bombardment, but otherwise he was unharmed. He had had worse.

Harry struggled to get to his feet.

Watson hurried over and gave him a hand. "Harry!"

Watson quickly began probing Harry's body. Harry shrugged him off. "I'm fine. Fine. Bruises are nothing and I'm surely quite glad that it's only bruises we seem to have incurred."

"And a few cuts," Challenger admitted, noticing the oozing of blood from his chin at that moment.

"And cuts," Harry added.

"This brings me to five!" Harry began his countdown again now that the interruption was past.

Everyone turned to him in disbelief.

"You mean there's more?" Conan demanded, still smoldering from Challenger's tease.

"We now know who had not only tricked and lulled us into complacency, but perhaps even learned why!" Harry explained.

"What?" Challenger asked.

"Yes, what?" Conan agreed. "I still feel as left out of this equation as before...except that now I ache all over my body. Body and..." He gave Challenger a pointed look. "...Soul."

Challenger looked down in shame.

Conan sighed, then went to Challenger and put an arm about his shoulder. "I'm sorry, old friend."

"Who are you calling old?" Challenger laughed.

"You!" Conan laughed back.

Watson looked once more at the spoiled sweet rolls. He started to bend down for one, but Harry stopped him. "Got more in the kitchen, Watson."

"Just reaching to tie my right shoe," Watson hurriedly explained.

Harry smiled and allowed Watson to pretend to tie his shoe, while he turned to the others.

"And sixth and final, as Holmes would say," Harry continued. "Shall now tell you who has sabotaged my crystal ball, been watching our activity not only here, but on the Master of the World, which Jules and Wells flew us back on; but also, whom we have previously met and engaged with."

Challenger's eyes rounded. "You mean...."

Harry nodded. "That's exactly who I mean," he agreed without allowing Challenger to finish. "And now we can determine a course of action based on what we know."

Watson and Conan exchanged blank looks and mouthed, "Who?"

Harry laughed. "Watson. Conan. Isn't it obvious who has done this?"

They both shook their heads.

And then Harry told them.

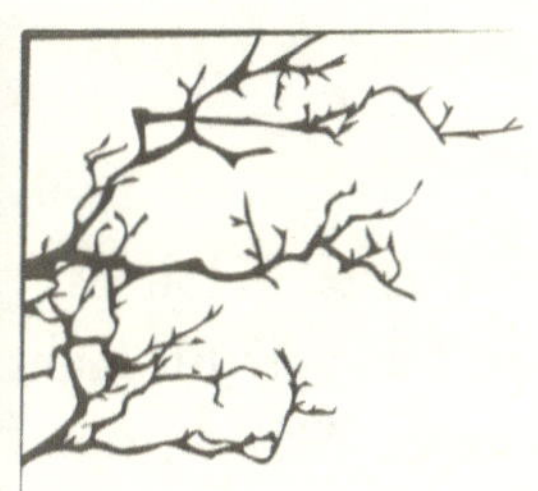

Baker Street

Watson climbed out of the Ford Tesla that Harry was driving and then waved goodbye to Challenger who sat in the back and then to Harry.

Harry droves away, leaving Watson standing before his home.

Watson sighed wearily.

He dreaded opening the door and climbing the stairs to the sitting room and finding no one there. Even the thought of seeing his beloved Ms. Hudson was not picking up his mood any.

Resigned to his fate, he took out his key and unlocked the front door. He had only managed two steps inside when he began sniffing the air.

His face lit up.

221B Baler Street

WATSON BURST INTO THE sitting room and shouted, "Holmes!"

Holmes sat near the fire, a blanket over his legs. He wore his night robe and was smoking his pipe. He waved it at Watson. "Watson, I was wondering when you'd show up again."

He glanced over at Ms. Hudson, seated in her usual corner, knitting. "Explained to Ms. Hudson that you were probably with Harry, Challenger and Conan deciding what to do next."

"Was!" Watson admitted, still surprised at Holmes not being more jubilant to see him.

"Surmised you would figure out what had been the source of the little trap that had been laid for us."

"We did. Well, actually Harry did."

Holmes smiled. "Good old Harry, I knew he would start practicing deduction more and stop leaning on his magic so heavily."

Holmes glanced at Watson a moment. "I see from looking at you that you were recently in a small explosion, you have bruises on your left side, as you landed on your right and the left was exposed."

Holmes rose and ventured closer to Watson. "By the look of your clothing and hair, I perceive that you were caught in a magical fire, as a real fire would have not just discolored your clothing and hair, as this has done."

He came closer still. "And judging by the number of small cuts on your face and hands..." He reached over and brushed a finger across Watson's right sleeve. "Glass crystal left on your clothing...which is of a rare glass found only in Germany and used exclusively by Harry in is séances...that the crystal ball exploded."

Watson's eyes rounded. "But...how?"

"Elementary, dear Watson. You and the others have concluded that the High Tea Society is behind this, have you not?"

"Yes, but..."

"And that the bargain that was made with them in San Francisco was not one to your benefit after all, but was a plot on their part to manipulate us all?"

"Yes, that's true, but..."

"And" Holmes stopped Watson's words with a gesture of his pipe. "You have realized that we now know where next to go and what steps must be taken to end the unholy alliance of the High Tea Society?"

"Yes, but..." Watson again tried to finish his sentence. But Holmes stopped him by clasping Watson with a hug.

"Truly glad you are unharmed, Watson."

Holmes let go and went back to his chair and began puffing on his pipe again.

Ms. Hudson looked up and smiled at Watson, who still looked battle shocked and surprised. "Set a plate of scones on the table for you, John and the tea is still warm. Sherlock told me to expect you any minute, so I had plenty of time to prepare it for you."

"But Holmes," Watson protested. "You never said you knew to the minute when I would arrive!"

Holmes smiled. "Really, Watson. You ask that now when Ms. Hudson has spread a delicious repast for you on the table."

"Blast you Holmes!" Watson cursed, and then he smiled. "It's good to have you back."

Holmes gave Watson a smile of such warmth that he almost staggered from the weight of it. "John, it is always a pleasure to be back. With you. But now, your scones are getting cold."

Watson looked at the table, then at Holmes, then at Ms. Hudson who grinned at him, and then at Holmes who gave him a friendly nod, then instead of arguing or grumbling, he hurried to the table and sat down. He grabbed a scone, lathered some butter on it, and then began eating it.

"Ah!" He exclaimed.

Ms. Hudson laughed.

"What's so blasted funny?" Watson demanded, eyeing her sternly.

"Sherlock said that would be the first thing you would say once you sat down at the table."

Watson started to make a sharp retort, but instead he fought off his negative emotions and went back to eating his scone. And to prove Watson is not fazed by the remark, he made an unintelligible, "Ar-hem!"

Holmes and Ms. Hudson both laughed.

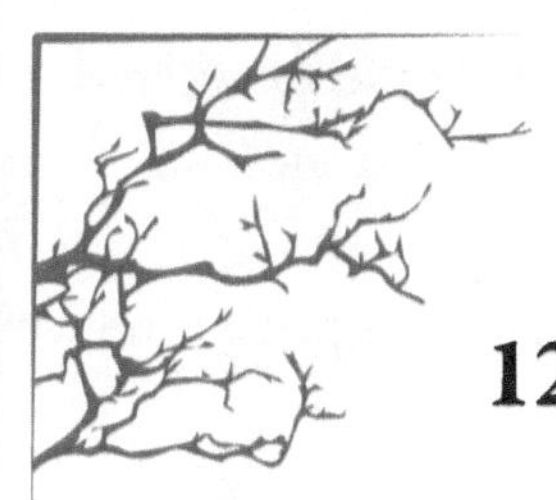

1212 Memory Lane

Three days later Harry stood at his window looking at Memory Lane below as Challenger and Conan climbed out of a cab. They looked up and waved. He nodded to them, and then he turned to look at his table once more.

Harry's room is repaired. It had cost him quite a bit on the repairs, but Lady Shareen had sent him three men out of work who needed the job and he had paid them quite well to finish quickly. They had. He had then paid them a month's wages in addition to their wages and expenses, to their surprise.

They had not heard that Harry was one of the sponsors of Lady Shareen's charitable organization that helped the poor and homeless. He did not tell them either. He did not spend his money on the charity to gain fame or notoriety; he already had that. He did it because he loved people.

Well, not everyone obviously, but enough that his good heartfelt empty if he did not contribute to the well-being of his fellow man.

A knock on his door.

He hurried downstairs to the door and opened it.

Challenger and Conan nodded and greeted him as they passed to the sitting room upstairs. "Harry. Harry." They greeted.

He greeted them back, waited until they passed, and then shut the door. He then put a magical ward upon it with a gesture of his right hand. For a moment, the door frame lit up a brilliant blue, and then it shimmered and faded away. But the seal was there, nonetheless. No one would be able to enter he did not so desire.

He climbed the stairs and saw both Conan and Challenger seated at the table, where a brand new and much larger crystal ball now sat on a throne of pure silver and gold.

"Friends, now that we know who our real enemies are, it's time we took action to stop them from further chicanery."

"Agree to that," Conan said.

"And I, most heartily," Challenger roared in his usually loud voice.

"But first..." Harry said. He waved his right hand and a glass of champagne, still bubbling appeared before each man at the table as well as his own self.

He sat at his usual place, raised his own glass, and made a toast. "To the new team."

Conan and Challenger both exchanged puzzled looks.

Harry grinned. "Oh, haven't I told you yet. I spoke to Holmes last night."

"And?" Challenger demanded.

"He agreed with me."

"On what?" Conan inquired, his eyebrows arching in surprise.

"That we make a good team."

Challenger snorted and waved a hand. "Of course, we do, any fool would be able to see that!"

Conan tittered behind his right hand.

Challenger glared at him.

Harry rose and raise his glass again, "To the Journey!"

Conan and Challenger rose and raised their own glasses.

"What journey?" Conan asked, plainly puzzled by the toast.

"Ours!" Harry exclaimed. "Our journey as a team to solve crime and bring supernatural villains and culprits to justice!"

"Here, here, Harry. That is a splendid idea," Challenger roared, "But I have an expedition planned on
the morrow."

Conan shook his own head. "And I have three operations and four stories to finish these next four days."

Harry smiled.

And neither Conan nor Challenger had the slightest idea of why he smiled like that as they joined his toast and drank their own champagne.

"To the Journey of Magic," Harry added and then said, "Of Magic and Logic."

"Here, here!" The others said in agreement.

"To Magic and logic!" They shouted.

Page |

Don't miss out!

Visit the website below and you can sign up to receive emails whenever John Pirillo publishes a new book. There's no charge and no obligation.

https://books2read.com/r/B-A-EMSD-GNIBC

BOOKS 2 READ

Connecting independent readers to independent writers.

Did you love *Sherlock Holmes Urban Fantasy Mysteries 4*? Then you should read *The Baker Street Universe*[1] by John Pirillo!

"I am dying!" Conan said to the Stranger who had come to him.

"No, you are not!" Professor Challenger told him. "This is just the beginning!"

In Victorian London, a doctor is dying.

And not just any doctor...but the late, great Sir Arthur Conan Doyle!

Before he passes on, he wants to make sure his wife is taken care of...

Shown just how much he truly loves and cares for her...

And finish his last Sherlock Holmes story, which will be his masterpiece!

---

1. https://books2read.com/u/bx1k0q

2. https://books2read.com/u/bx1k0q

And in another Victorian London, existing on a parallel world in a parallel universe to ours, there are heroes, heroes who exist in a world of magic and Steampunk science.

They have other plans for Conan.

To rescue him.

From death!

A deeply moving portrayal of the late Sir Arthur Conan Doyle which digs deeply into the lore about him and connects him intimately with the very characters he's written in a new universe...one of many which parallel our own.

Conan is going to be given a choice few of us are ever given...

The choice to pass on from life or to continue living...

In another universe...

The Baker Street Universe!

Where he has the chance to be part of the Sherlock Holmes team and to make friends who are true heroes, just like the ones he has written.

And even more exciting for him is the knowledge that if he does cross over into this new universe, he will be alive during the most exciting time of history!

Every writer that ever lived.

Every character that every writer has ever written.

All will be alive and existing in this parallel universe!

An Urban Fantasy Sherlock Holmes mystery novel.

Take a heartwarming and fun ride through the minds of Sir Arthur Conan Doyle, Sherlock Holmes, Watson, and so many others you have read about, but never seen in such vivid detail.

Buy your book now.

Read more at www.johnpirillo.com.

Also by John Pirillo

Angel Hamilton
Broken Fangs

Baker Street Universe Tales
Baker Street Universe Tales
Baker Street Universe Tales 2
Baker Street Universe Tales 3
Baker Street Universe Tales 4
Baker Street Universe Tales 5
Baker Street Universe Tales Seven

Between
Prince of Between

"Classic Baker Street Universe Sherlock Holmes"
Sherlock Holme: Hyde's Night of Terror
Case of the Deadly Goddess
Case of the Abominable

Detective Judge Dee
Detective Dee Murder Most Chaste

Elektron
Elektron

Escape To Adventure
Escape to Adventure

Hollow Earth Special Forces
Hollow Earth Special Forces, Forbidden World

Holmes
Sherlock Holmes Struck
Sherlock Holmes A Dangerous Act

Mystery Knight
HellBound Mystery
Hell Bound Angel

PhaseShift

PhaseShift
PhaseShift Two: Crossover
PhaseShift: Shifting Worlds

Rocketman
Rocketman
Rocket Man, Mission Berlin
Rocketman Christmas
Rocket Man, Sky Commando
Time Wars

Sherlock Holmes
Sherlock Holmes, ICE
The Ice Man
Sherlock Holmes Fallen
Sherlock Holmes: Monster
Sherlock Holmes: Tick Tock
Sherlock Holmes Christmas Magic
Sherlock Holmes Dark Secret
Sherlock Holmes Shadow of Dorian Gray
Sherlock Holmes Vampire
Sherlock Holmes: Cursed in Stone
Sherlock Holmes Apparition
Sherlock Holmes Case of the Raging Madness
Sherlock Holmes Dark Princess
Sherlock Holmes Dark Angel
Constable Evans' Fancy
Sherlock Holmes Matter of Perception
Sherlock Holmes Tangled
Sherlock Holmes Case of the Gossamer Lady

Sherlock Holmes House of Shadows
Sherlock Holmes The Yellow Death
Sherlock Holmes Oblique
Sherlock Holmes Mystery Train Winter Collection
Sherlock Holmes A Tale Less Told
Sherlock Holmes Mystery Six
Sherlock Holmes, Rules of Darkness, Special Edition
Sherlock Holmes Shape of Justice
Sherlock Holmes Christmas Magic
Sherlock Holmes Fallen Angel
Ghostly Shadows
Sherlock Holmes: Artifact
Sherlock Holmes Bloody Hell
Sherlock Holmes Monster of the Tower
Sherlock Holmes Darkest of Nights
Sherlock Holmes Nightmare
Sherlock Holmes Poetry of Death
Sherlock Holmes, Dracula
Sherlock Holmes #3, Ice Storm

Sherlock Holmes Urban Fantasy Mysteries
Sherlock Holmes Urban Fantasy Mysteries 2
Sherlock Holmes Urban Fantasy Mysteries 3
Sherlock Holmes Urban Fantasy Mysteries 4
Sherlock Holmes, The Dracula Files
Sherlock Holmes, Dark Clues
Sherlock Holmes, Case of the Undying Man
Sherlock Holmes, Mystery of the Sea
Sherlock Holmes, Night Watch
Sherlock Holmes, Mystery of the Path not Taken
Sherlock Holmes, the Dorian Gray Affair

The Baker Street Universe
Sherlock Holmes, The Dracula Affair
Baker Street Universe Tales 6
Spector

The Baker Street Detective
Strange Times, The Baker Street Detective, Book2
The Baker Street Detective, Hollow Man

Standalone
Sherlock Holmes Deadly Consequences
Invisibility Factor
Red Painted Souls
Between
Robin Hood
Shadow Man
The Rainbow Bridge
Cartoon, Johnnie Angel
Sherlock Holmes 221B
Sherlock Holmes Shape Shifter
Urban Fantasy Mysteries
Sherlock Holmes, Urban Fantasy Mysteries
Romancing the Word

Watch for more at www.johnpirillo.com.